The Gr

Stephanie Parker

Grimoire Books

Published in 2010 by Grimoire Books
A Punked Books/Authortrek imprint

Grimoire Books
C/O Authortrek
PO Box 54168
London
W5 9EE
(FAQ via www.authortrek.com/punked-books)

Contents

*To my parents, for moving me to the edge of the woods
and letting me find the magic.*

Chapter 1

It seemed perfectly normal that the chestnut tree was laughing and reaching in through Charlotte's window. It offered a branch for her to walk out of her window, and made steps to the ground. A warm wind, which smelled of something much nicer than normal wind blew in, turned back her duvet and blew her hair around. Charlotte stood up and the wind pushed her to the window.

She put her foot on the branch. The wind began to blow faster and faster, blowing her down the branch, down to the ground. The garden looked different and a curious man was standing at the edge, calling her by her name.

She was afraid. She turned to run back up the tree into her room but the tree had raised its branches high, she couldn't get back.... She ran to the house but she couldn't find her own front door.

She raced around to the back door... not there! Around and around she ran, calling "Mum... Dad... Mum..." All the time the man just stood in the garden, and then she realised that he was someone she knew, but she didn't know who. Suddenly the house and the garden were gone. Charlotte was in a wood, and there was a fire coming. There was a wall around the trees, and tall gates. She hammered at the gates to warn the man about the fire, but she couldn't get inside. She ran, ran, kept running. The man was gone but she couldn't get back into the woods and the fire was coming closer and closer, she had to warn him... But then the dream faded.

She woke up, and it was morning. Outside the window the tree stood in sunlight, strong, and safe and just like any old tree. As she walked back to bed, she trod on something smooth, bent down and picked up a long leaf with little pointy bits around it – a chestnut leaf.

When all these things I am about to tell you happened, Charlotte was eleven - nearly twelve. She had long, gangly arms and legs, lots red hair and also freckles. She was skinnier than she'd like to be and taller than most of her friends in the new town – although she'd been shorter than most of her London friends, which she thought was pretty strange.

Charlotte and her family had just moved down from London. They had bought a beautiful old house just outside of the town where her Nan lived. Once, a long long time ago, said her mother, the house had been owned by her mother's great, great great, greatgreatgreat grandmother or someone, so really, it wasn't a new house at all.

Charlotte's Nan had found the house years ago while she was looking up the family history, and when it came up for sale she had told Charlotte's Mum. They'd been thinking about leaving London for a few years and since it wasn't too far away, it seemed like perfect timing. Even the sale had gone really smoothly, 'like magic', Charlotte's Mum had said.

By the time they had sold their house in London and bought this one (bought it *back* thought Charlotte), there was only a few months left of school before the summer holidays, so she had to move schools right at the end of the year. It was okay meeting new people and she had already emailed all her friends planning visits, but she still missed everyone.

The day her family arrived at the new house was a beautiful, sunny day in late spring. April flowers bloomed in the banks by the road; cow parsley and hogweed clogged the hedgerows and flowers cluttered up all remaining space. The air smelt of animals and blossoms.

Their car wound up a narrow road and turned right down a long twisted driveway. It was an old car and it spluttered down the hill like a farting heap of old metal, scaring birds out of the grass. Charlotte's Dad had had the car since he was at university, which was a very long time ago indeed. It was really rusty and embarrassing, and every time it went for its MOT Charlotte hoped it would fail.

This time, the only thing it passed was something that Charlotte thought was a herd of deer, but at the noise they ran into the woods at the edge of the fields. She wasn't sure she'd really seen them so she didn't say anything, but something had moved into the woods, lots of *fast* things.

As the car slowed down in clouds of smoke, the house came into sight - old, square, medium sized and made from grey stone. There were two small barns in front, and between them a garden enclosed by a stone wall. In the bottom wall was an iron gate leading from the garden down into the field below. Beside the driveway was an old shed, and behind the house were a raggedy bunch of old apple trees.

There was a big old chestnut tree in the front of the house, outside the end window. Beyond that was another small garden plot which someone had ploughed but not planted, so weeds covered the dirt. The car squeaked to a stop, and after a few splutters, they could finally hear the silence outside the windows.

"Wow," said Charlotte, "is this really it?" It looked much bigger than she was expecting, much bigger than the London house. Maybe that would make up for being in the country. She had spent summers with her Nan before, it was okay but she'd been kind of bored. She was hoping her parents would let her take the train to London to visit her friends on weekends; it wasn't so far away really.

"What do you think?" said her dad, Mr. Enright. "Quite something, isn't it?"

She snapped back from her daydream of ordering sandwiches and arriving in London on her own train. "Sure is... there's no-one for miles!"

"Not exactly," said her mother, "I mean, we passed another driveway right before our own, their house is hidden right behind that hill there." She pointed to the hill behind the house. Charlotte turned to look, and sure enough, just at the very top of the hill she could glimpse the tops of some trees, and yes... the corner of a chimney, about a quarter of a mile away or less. Quite close, really.

"And," continued Mrs. Enright, "the man who sold us this house said they have a couple of kids around your age, hopefully you'll be able to get along with them just fine."

Her father straightened up and breathed in a huge lungful of air. "Smell that. You can small how good the air is."

"You can smell animals too," said Charlotte. "I hope the wind blows the other way once in a while." She wrinkled her nose more than she had to. She really didn't mind the smell too much. It smelt mostly of hay and straw and cow feed. Not too horrible. Not as bad as the car, the smoke from which was disgusting, like something out of a pollution video.

Charlotte could see the offending cow sheds, across the little valley in front of the house. To see them the family had to crane their heads around the barn by the front garden.

Behind the barn the fields plunged down a hill and back up again, rolling away and away into more hills, hills that would eventually lead right to the ocean, about ten miles away. The cow sheds were just over the hill across the first valley.

"Could we go and see the farm?" They all turned to look at the top of the sheds across the way.

"In a few days, maybe," said her dad. "Let's get unpacked and settled in first. Last one in the house is a Tweenie". Charlotte rolled her eyes and walked. "Want to see your room?" he called back, and she whizzed past him, sliding to a halt on the wood floor inside the door, laughing. Her mother puffed in through the door behind her and her father came in last shouting, "Not fair, not fair, Mary, you cheated!" Her mother laughed. "She pushed me!" he tried to explain to Charlotte, who was already going upstairs with her mother, giggling.

Charlotte's mother opened up a door at the end of the upstairs hallway.

"We thought this could be your room. There's four bedrooms, Dad and I picked the biggest because we are the biggest, and you really have the choice of the others, but I liked this room most."

"So do I," said Charlotte. "It's got a big closet and everything." It also had two windows, one looking out over the front lawn and the barn, and the other looking from the side of the house out across a small wooded valley. The view from the front window was partially obscured by the large, old chestnut tree Charlotte had seen from the driveway, whose branches brushed the window once in a while in the wind.

"We'll have to trim that tree. "Just in case of a high wind. Don't want you waking up covered in broken glass, now, do we?" said Mrs. Enright before she popped back downstairs.

Charlotte looked at the tree for the first time. It was very beautiful. She bet herself she could climb it. Maybe they could even build a tree house. She suddenly felt that she didn't want them to trim the tree, in fact that it was very important that the tree stay just the way it was.

The room began to feel as if something warm had come in behind her, and a lovely smell came in. Must be through the window, she thought, although it was shut.

She could see over the top of the barn to the field below and all the way to the edge of the woods.

The skin on her arms began to rise and she realised with a start that someone was standing in the field looking right up at her. She shrank back from the window, then felt silly – of course they couldn't see into the window from that far away. She looked again but they'd gone.

Her mother bustled in behind her with her suitcase. "Most of your stuff is already in here. Some of it is probably in that enormous pile of boxes in the living room. It's going to take a while. You want to unpack, or explore?"

"Explore please."

"Alright," her mother consulted her watch. "Don't go too far..." but Charlotte had already gone.

Charlotte rocketed down the stairs and out into the sun. They'd had to drive for four hours that morning and she'd been cramped up in the backseat in mountains of suitcases and bedding. In fact, they'd spent the last month packing and packing and packing. Each day she'd come home from school and not be able to find something else, it was SO annoying.

She walked over to the chestnut tree. It was very big. The

branches stretched thick and heavy, out, out... out... She looked, and could see the branch that brushed her window. If only it were closer to the house, she thought. I could climb right into my bedroom window. But it wasn't, and besides, the branch was too thin to even support a squirrel. Not even a branch really, more of a long twig.

She wandered around the back of the house, finding bits of old machinery in the grass behind the shed, and then walked into the front garden, clambered on top of the wall and sat down.

"Wow", she thought. The field below the garden went down to a small stream and then up again to the cow sheds. What made Charlotte think "wow" was the wood that started partway down the hill to the right, covered the slope and spread out down the valley for ages and ages.

This, she thought, was the wood she could see from her bedroom windows. It was huge. She could see a small path close to the bottom, and standing on the path was what looked like a green man . Charlotte gasped and stayed very still. Even from far away she could see that his skin was quite green and that it was rough, like wood. He looked back at her, still and quiet. The skin on her back crawled as if ants were walking over it and then she realized she was looking right at a deer. Not a green man, a deer. She blinked. Definitely a deer, a big one with greyish fur.

She turned and yelled, "Hey Dad, I can see a deer from here!" But when she turned around to look again, it had gone. "What?" yelled her Father from behind a pile of boxes by the car "Pardon? I couldn't quite hear you."

"I saw a deer, but it's gone now," she shouted.

"Deer? Don't yell, you'll scare it away," he bellowed back

"Too late," she said.

"What?"

"Never mind," she made a big waving motion - *nothing*.

As her Dad bent to pick up a suitcase, she decided to go through the gate into the field, and walk into the wood a small way. She looked back to signal where she was going, but her father was disappearing into the house.

The edge of the wood was cool and smelt rich with dirt and leaves and flowers. Big clumps of moss were growing on rocks, the ferns and underbrush rustled. Light streamed in through the trees, and she saw a bright carpet of blue down a path to her left and went running down the slope towards it. Bluebells, lots of them. Bluebells as high as her knees, swaying gently. She bent down and pulled at one. The stem slid out easily. She bent down and started picking. She wandered around, getting farther and farther into the wood.

The wood began to fill up with tall oak and beech trees and got darker. Charlotte had wandered towards a dark, knotty looking mound, about ten feet high. It looked like a very old tree, or the remains of one. Rotten wood was covered with ferns, ivy wound around it, draped off the sides. On top, years and years of dead leaves had decayed into good soil, and some small saplings had grown up. Other things grew on the mound too, shelves of flat-topped fungus sprung from the sides going all the way up. It was massive, much bigger than she had thought and just when she was thinking of putting down the flowers and climbing on top of it, she suddenly felt a prickle at the back of her neck.

It ran down to the bottom of her spine, and then the woods went very quiet. She got frightened. She thought she saw something out of the corner of her eye. She looked, startled, her heart pumping. Nothing. Nothing there. Nothing at all. She turned around slowly, looking everywhere. Was she being watched? It felt like something was behind her, looking at her from the mound. Slowly her stomach spiralled out and down and she just knew she had to move.

She backed slowly to the main path and then ran like mad out of the woods and back up the hill. She didn't stop running until she reached the garden wall, and clambered up the lowest part, throwing her flowers up first and diving over, scraping her knees and finally crouching, out of breath, on the safe side.

She peeked over the top. Nothing there. Of course. Dozy. I'm so stupid, she thought. Getting spooked in a wood. It was probably just a fox. She turned around, but she couldn't

11

see her parents, although she could hear her father calling through the house to her mother. She gathered her flowers and walked up to the kitchen door.

"Lovely," sighed her mother. "Where on earth did you go to get those?"

"The wood over the garden wall," she said. "It's full of them."

"You're not supposed to pick them you know. Maybe later on we can all go for a walk together, I'd love to see them. After we've done some more unpacking, though. We've got to eat out of bowls today, the box with the plates in it is at the bottom! And it's going to be sandwiches again for supper if I can't find the pots and pans." She stopped. "Look at you. You've skinned your knees. I know we have bandages somewhere...".

The next evening Charlotte went for a walk with her parents and couldn't figure out why she'd been so scared. The wood was bright, and filled with beautiful secrets. There were streams, a ruined house, blackberry brambles at the edges, ("No berries until September," said her mother) and a perfectly circular clearing with a stream running next to it... paradise. Once, she thought she saw the green man again, and was looking for the deer when the man just... turned... into a tree trunk, and she realized she'd been looking at a stump covered in moss the whole time.

Unpacking took the rest of the week, and the following Monday she had to start at her new school. When they wrote to the school to register her they were told that there was a dress code. Everyone had to wear blue or grey, and no jeans were allowed. Furthermore, girls were expected to wear skirts – although the headmaster said it was ok to wear trousers if they really wanted.

"I don't want to wear a skirt," said Charlotte, but her mother insisted on buying her a grey one anyway, as well as navy trousers.

"But they're UGLY," moaned Charlotte, "grey is UGLY. NAVY is UGLY. Why can't I wear pink, or purple, or green, why just Blue and Grey. I HATE blue and grey. Why not even black?"

"We'll see," sighed her mother. "Just start off like this, please?"

And so Charlotte started off. Her father drove her to school the first day, but told her that after that she was going to have to take the bus. "The bus will be fine. It goes close to the house," he said. "Most of the children from this area take it."

They went into the secretary's office and her father said goodbye.

Her first class was history, and immediately she wished she was back at home.

Her teacher's name was Mr. Green, and he took Charlotte aside before class and talked to her. "Charlotte, this is class 2-1. Here are some books you'll need, come and talk to me after class and we'll see where you stand. All right everyone, this is Charlotte Enright. She's going to be coming to this school from now on."

"Where should I sit?" she asked, as he hadn't pointed out a chair.

Someone giggled, a small dark-haired girl sitting half way back in the classroom.

"Stop that, Rosemary," said the teacher. "You can sit behind Rosemary," said Mr. Green, "and Rosemary, you can help Charlotte find her way around the school for a while."

Rosemary didn't necessarily look too pleased about this, but she said, "Yes sir," anyway.

After class Mr. Green ordered Rosemary to wait outside the door and show her to the next class.

"My school in London was twice as big as this," Charlotte told Rosemary.

"Good, well you won't need me then," said Rosemary. Rosemary was shorter than Charlotte, and had brown hair to Charlotte's auburn. She was a little plump but not very, and looked a lot older than she was. She wore very tight blue trousers. She looked at Charlotte like she was a bit cross.

"I'm sorry, I only meant... I mean, thanks for showing me around. You don't have to if you really don't want to..."

13

"Nah, it's OK," said Rosemary, "I don't mind really."

Is it really alright to wear trousers?" asked Charlotte looking at Rosemary, "I hate skirts."

"Yeah," said Rosemary, "Only the boring girls wear skirts."

"Good," said Charlotte, "I'm going to burn mine."

"Really," said Rosemary, "you're really going to burn it?" She looked delighted, and Charlotte decided that she was probably quite nice really.

They reached the classroom door, and Charlotte just raised her eyebrows and smiled. Rosemary smiled back, and then they went in.

In the playground later a tall blond girl came up to her. "So you're the new girl from London then?"

"Yes, I am."

"I go to London all the time with my Mum. We go shopping every month, there's nothing to buy in town, it's horrible here. Where was your favourite shop?"

"Uh, I like Oxford Street..."

"Eugh," said the other girl wrinkling her nose. "We NEVER go there. We only go to Knightsbridge. You can only buy horrible things on Oxford Street. Is that where you bought those horrible shoes, on Oxford Street?" she sneered. "I bet you come from somewhere nasty, don't you?"

Charlotte just looked at her and was about to say something really clever about Selfridges being on Oxford street and really quite good when Rosemary came up and said, "Go away Nancy, you've only been to London twice in your life you liar."

"More than you," sniffed Nancy, and stalked off to sit with her friends. Rosemary introduced her to Julia and Elizabeth, other girls in the group - none of them wore skirts and they all seemed very friendly.

"That's Nancy Kettering and her friends," said Elizabeth. "They're horrible. They play kiss chase with the boys all the time and pretend to be really grown up. Her father has a big car and he owns a shop in town, so she thinks she's really big."

"We hate her," added Rosemary. "She's really mean, too, so don't be her friend".

"I hate her too," said Charlotte.

"She went to Julia's birthday party last year and cheated at all the games. She spilled punch on her dress and told her Dad that Julia's mother had done it."

They looked over at Nancy's gang, who looked back and stuck out their tongues.

Later on, in English class, the teacher was making them read *The Lion the Witch and the Wardrobe*, which Charlotte had read a hundred times at least; and she had the DVD. She started doodling trees in the margins of her binder.

"Charlotte, are you paying any attention at all?" The English teacher was a sharp-faced woman with short dark hair, and she was looking right at Charlotte. One of the girls in Nancy's gang tittered.

"Yes Miss Stevens." Charlotte went red – her first day and already she was being shouted at by the teacher.

"Good. Then you can tell me exactly what happens next."

Charlotte told her.

"Now, can you do me a favour and LOOK like you're paying attention."

"Yes, Miss Stevens." But Charlotte was not paying attention. She was thinking of what had happened a few days ago.

Her father had gone out for a while and come back with a strange look on his face. He told her to go and get his slippers, which was odd but she went up to get them.

On the way back down the stairs she heard a sharp sound, muffled by the door, and heard her mother laughing. She opened the door and saw her father lying face down on the floor, holding a cord that went behind the couch. He was laughing hysterically. Her mother sat on the back of the couch trying to push something out from behind it, laughing also. They saw her come in and laughed even harder, her father letting go of the cord and sitting up.

She started to giggle at them then her mother pushed a medium sized brown dog from behind the couch where it was hiding.

"It's a surprise!" said her Dad. "We thought you'd like to have a dog. It's from the RSPCA. He's almost a year old and his name's Roger." At the sound of his name Roger looked up. He was sprawling in a half sit, with his head really low, obviously nervous.

"He was really friendly," said Mr. Enright, getting up from the floor. "Give him a moment, the car ride scared him."

Charlotte put out her hand. Roger sniffed it, wagged his tail almost once and then licked the proffered fingers tentatively. She stroked his head and he quieted down a bit. They made a big fuss of him, fed him and he settled in front of the empty fireplace and watched them from between his feet.

Later on, after supper she had taken him for a walk in the woods, on a leash so he wouldn't run away and get lost. The evenings were getting longer and it was still quite sunny. Roger stopped and sniffed everything.

With him, Charlotte decided that she felt quite safe, so she didn't mind when the dog pulled on the leash, leading her further into the woods.

They stumbled through into the clearing that she had seen when she was walking with her parents. On the way in, Charlotte got stung by a stinging nettle. There were loads of them, she realised, all around the clearing. They almost looked like someone had planted them there to keep people out.

Inside, Charlotte looked around. It was surrounded by big chestnut trees with spreading branches. Charlotte counted them, there were twelve and they all looked the same. It would be easy to get lost from here, she thought with a small tremor. If you didn't know which way you'd come in. She took her bearing from the stream in the middle. "I came in between the second and third tree to the right of where the stream comes in," she thought, but stuck a twig into the ground just to make sure. Roger had stopped, finally and was sitting down and panting, smelling the air. She looked at him and smelt the air with him.

"The air does smell different in here," she thought.

Sweeter. Spicy. Warmer. "Like, I don't know," she wondered, "baking? Roses? Sweet Peas? Hay?" Grasshoppers chirped in the long grass, there were a few primroses on the edge and lots of soft grass in the middle.

The trees were bigger and older than the one by the house. They were in flower, the small candles of flowers fragrant and beautiful. They seemed magical. The trunks on the shady sides were caked thick with soft green moss, and inside the clearing, thick roots snaked into the ground. It was a moment of great peace. The two of them, girl and dog, wandered over to the stream, and Roger waded right in and started drinking.

She went up stream a few feet from the dog and cupped some water for herself. It was sweet and thirst quenching. It tasted a little of the way the clearing smelled, and also with another, deeper, slightly earthy taste. It was so good, and perfectly clear. She drank some more. She was just about to take her fourth drink when Roger barked.

Charlotte grabbed his leash just in time just in time to stop him jumping out of reach. From the corner of her eye she saw movement. She whirled around and the man in the corner of her eye turned once more into a deer; or rather, a grey-brown stag with large antlers. It looked her right in the eye for a second or less before Roger barked again and tried to run towards it. The deer turned and ran away so fast, Charlotte could barely believe it had even been there.

The school bell rang and Charlotte jumped back into the class. "Class, please have this book read all the way through for next Monday," Mrs. Stevens was saying, as the boys and girls shoved their books away and hurried out the door.

It was the chestnut tree again. It was laughing and reaching in through Charlotte's window. It offered its branch to her, and made steps to the ground. The wind, the sweet smelling wind turned back her duvet and blew her nightdress around. Her dress grew longer and longer and bigger and bigger until it filled the room. Charlotte stood up, fighting her way

17

through the folds of fabric and walked to the window.

Again, she walked down the tree to the ground. Again, the man was standing at the edge of the garden, which looked the same as it had before – completely different than in real life.

She was sure she knew the man, as well as if he had been her father, her brother, herself. She stood silently, watching him.

She woke up and it was morning. The window was closed, and her nightdress was just the normal size it usually was and she had another chestnut leaf in her bed. She put it on her night table, beside the first one and she lay back and waited for her Mother to come and wake her up.

Chapter 2

One day while out walking Roger, Charlotte finally met the boy from next door, although she'd already seen him at school ("That's Ken Stone," Rosemary had said "He's like your next door neighbour, you know, if your houses were on a normal street and not in fields and stuff").

They looked warily at each other and he shoved out his hand to introduce himself and after a few moments of awkward talk, Roger jumped up and slavered all over Ken, breaking the ice. As they laughed, he seemed to come to a decision and beckoned her into a tunnel in the undergrowth which she hadn't noticed. They struggled through to a little cave beneath the thorns – they had to crawl in and sit down to get inside, but from there, they could see the woods around without being seen themselves.

Ken was the same age, or a little older than herself and quite nice. He told her some stories about the woods. He said that according to his Mum there were fairies living in amongst the trees. He said that once in a while they were supposed to come and try to take a child from the area and substitute it for one of their own. These children, he told her, are called 'changelings' and the fairy child grows up as the child of the family, while their child grows up in fairyland not knowing who he or she really is.

Then he got a very strange look on his face and said, "I used to think I was a changeling."

"Why?" asked Charlotte, dying of curiosity.

"Because changelings are supposed to feel different than everyone else, like they belong somewhere else and I feel more at home in the woods than anywhere else."

"If you're a changeling, why do you look just like a normal person?" she asked, thinking he was a bit mad.

"Because," he said, "they're not really fairies, they're just like us, except they live inside the wood, somehow..." he paused, then he changed the subject.

"I was born here," he said. "In my house. My mother was born here too. My Great-Grandfather bought the house - he

19

was pretty interesting. No one knows where he came from, and when he was older he went for a walk one day and never came home. No one knows where he went, either. People thought he got lost or something, they looked for ages and ages, but he was so old... He went out without a jacket or anything the day after my Great-Grandmother died."

"That's so sad," said Charlotte.

"Yeah, I guess my Gran was really upset, losing both her parents in two days. My Mum still remembers it." Just then a rabbit wandered into sight and they stopped talking, but it hopped away anyway.

"I see lots of animals like this," Ken said. "Sometimes I come here to read. In the autumn you can reach through the thorns and pick berries. I have to trim it back in the summer or my tunnel grows over."

"What kind of animals have you seen?" she asked him.

"Badgers, sometimes foxes and lots of rabbits. Quite often I've seen deer. There's a herd of them living in the woods. You'd never know it, but once I saw a whole lot of them, they were grazing about twenty feet away, ten or eleven of them. There's one big one, an old stag with big horns. He's incredible. I've only seen him once or twice. He's grey too, not brown like the others."

Charlotte's Mother, Mrs. Enright, was a small, strong woman. She was a few pounds over-weight but didn't look it. She had brown hair which had been red when she was a child and she had just started finding grey strands in it which she would pull out with a shriek. She was pretty good at saying the right thing, and she and Charlotte were good friends.

"It's lovely here, Charlotte, don't you think?" she asked Charlotte one day, a few weeks after they had settled in.

"It's alright," said Charlotte, who still missed London and all her friends. "It's different for you, you don't have to go to school or meet all kinds of new people."

"Rubbish," answered Mrs. Enright. "You've already met

20

Ken, and I've saw his mother Iris for coffee just the other morning. You've got Rosemary too, you're doing fine. Besides, you spend half your evenings on the internet chatting with your friends in London, you can't possibly be lonely."

"I know," sighed Charlotte. Roger!" she called, and the dog came trotting over. "I'm going for a walk, be back soon."

"OK, dinner in a few hours so don't be late."

Charlotte was spending a lot of time in the woods with Roger, and sometimes when she was lying in the clearing, she thought she could hear voices, but she could never figure out if they were really there or not.

After school, she would study for an hour and take Roger for a walk after supper.

Ken knew there was something in the woods, but he just couldn't be sure what it was. He had spent most of his time in the past few years looking for it, crouching for hours in silence, watching. Sometimes he was looking at a badger den, sometimes rabbits, sometimes he was just watching.

He was sitting on a log eating a sandwich when Charlotte came up to him from around a tree.

"I've seen him," she said.

"Seen who?"

"Your big grey deer."

"Where?" asked Ken, his face suddenly serious.

"Last week, in the clearing down the other side of the hill. And the day we arrived too."

"Really?"

"I'm sure, he was huge, really big horns. He was grey, too, not like the other deer."

"They're called antlers. The spikes on them are called tines. You're supposed to be able to tell how old a deer is by counting them. You're lucky, he's a hard'un to spot." They sat for a while, looking around the area.

"I thought I saw a man in here the other day but then he disappeared... is it safe in here?"

21

"Probably just someone from town."

"Probably. Anyway, I've got to go," said Charlotte, finally. "I'm supposed to be back in time for tea. See you later".

"Suit yourself," said Ken. "See you later."

She grabbed Roger's leash and started running. "Race you home!" she said to the dog, and they ran over the hill and up to the garden.

Ken sort of liked Charlotte, at least she spent her time properly, not hanging around the boys like the other girls did. Mind you, Ken wasn't much like the other boys, either. He had a gang of friends, and he was on the football team, but he preferred to spend his spare time in the wood. He knew most of it inside out.

He had his own private place in the woods, the ruined house that Charlotte had seen once before. It was originally a gamekeeper's hut back when there were pheasants raised in the woods. Now, it was just four walls with a gap where the door used to be.

He wandered over to it, waiting for Charlotte to be out of sight. He didn't really want her coming to his hut, he wasn't sure why. He clambered through the ferns and into the tiny clearing where the remains of the house sat. He startled a few rabbits from the little pitch that used to be the garden. He sat down, pulled out his penknife and started to work on a small carving of a deer he was making.

He would often lie for hours with his head pillowed on a moss-covered stone, looking up at the trees and daydreaming. Sometimes he would fall asleep and have very strange and wonderful dreams.

It was Friday. With only four weeks of school to go Charlotte was buried in homework. Rosemary walked her to the bus stop after school. "I heard Ken Stone's after you!" she smirked

"No, he's not. He's just my neighbour."

"He told Elizabeth's brother that he likes you because you like to walk in his bloody woods. He's bonkers over those woods, he is. Thinks he's a pixie or something."

"They're haunted, those woods you know," she went on. "Once when I was smaller I thought I saw a green man in there, and he caught me looking at him. When I looked again, he was gone. He's supposed to be Robin Hood, or something."

"I thought Robin Hood was from Nottingham?" said Charlotte.

"Yeah, well he's like Robin Hood. He's got all kinds of made-up names. My Granddad called him the Green King."

"I think I may have seen him…" said Charlotte slowly, her mind whirling over the times she thought she'd seen the Green King. Should she be afraid? She didn't feel scared of the woods at all, not since the first time.

"He's supposed to steal children... or something. Young virgins!" snickered Rosemary. "Although the only one ever to go missing in there was that James Starling boy."

"Who's he?"

"He lives next door to you – other side from Ken! You're surrounded by weirdos, watch out, that's all I have to say."

The bus came and Charlotte waved goodbye.

She decided not to go to the wood that evening, and instead lay on her stomach under the chestnut tree in front of the house, with her maths homework in front of her. She was behind and was only allowed to go out as long as she stayed where her mother could see her. She had fifty problems to get through and she was only at number 13.

As she lay under the tree she got the feeling again that she was being watched. The air smelled sweet suddenly, like inside the clearing, and she felt very peaceful and relaxed.

She looked up cautiously from her book and there, standing on the wall at the bottom of the garden, was the Green King. She froze, and her heartbeat felt as if it was going to pound through her head. He was beckoning her to join him. She shook her head slightly not knowing what to do. He laughed and disappeared. She waited to see if he'd come back, but he didn't.

Her mother came out of the house. "Well," said Mrs. Enright. "You're going to have to do at least up to number 25 tonight. Maybe you should come inside."

"But..."

"I'm sorry, but otherwise you'll be spending your whole weekend working on maths and won't get anything else done. You spend so much time with that dog or walking in the woods with Ken that you're going to fail school if you don't buck up. Anyway, come in for tea."

After tea she worked another hour and was on number 22. "These are so boring!" she cried. "They take so long and I KNOW all this stuff." She was frustrated and unhappy and wasn't allowed out because she'd been so bad tempered. Her father leapt at the chance to take Roger for a walk. 'That dog's spoiled', she thought. 'He gets to have more fun than me. He doesn't have to do any stupid math homework.' Her mother wouldn't even help her check her mistakes. She had to go over each one two or three times to make sure it was alright.

She laboured long over the homework, occasionally mopping up a stray tear of self-pity and texting her old friends to tell them how much she hated her new school. Her father came back in and Roger lay down under the table with a sigh, wishing he'd had a longer walk.

Time passed. She kept looking out of the window in case the man came back, and sure enough, after an hour of homework she saw something outside. Creeping through the top gate of the garden were several young people. At first she thought they were from the town and she was about to call for her father, but even in the evening light she could see that they were green. She began to feel very excited, and scared.

A girl, who looked to be her own age, crept up to the window and peered in. She smiled at Charlotte, and motioned for her to come outside. Charlotte wanted to get up to go to the door, but just then her father came down from his study.

24

Her skin was tingling all over from excitement, it was like a movie, or a story, it just wasn't real. Ken must be right, these must be pixies. She couldn't believe what she was seeing; she actually pinched herself because she'd read somewhere that's what people do when they think they're dreaming. It hurt and her skin went red. She looked at her homework. She wasn't dreaming... She heard a noise.

"Thought I saw some deer outside," said her Dad who was behind her suddenly. "I just came down to tell you to look quietly." They both looked out of the window and there was nothing to be seen.

"Dad," said Charlotte "I've done most of my homework," and indeed she'd managed to get all the way to number 31, "can I go out for a while, please?"

Her father looked down at her, and ran his hand through his hair. "Alright. Just don't go off the property, alright? It's getting late."

"Alright!" she said "Thanks Dad!" She put her books away quickly and, pulling on a jacket, she ran outside and down to the bottom of the lawn to sit on the wall overlooking the woods.

She didn't feel at all afraid of the pixies, or whatever they were, although she knew she should be. What if they took her and put a changeling in her place? She tried to feel afraid, but she just felt so happy.

She climbed up the stones to the top of the wall and looked across the valley and up to the cow sheds at the top of the hill. The cows were still grazing. 'That must be where the boy who went missing lives,' she thought.

All the spring and summer flowers were out in the fields and the hedgerows. There were so many flowers. There were primroses, celandines, violets, bugles, dead nettles that looked like stinging nettles but with pale yellow flowers, there were elder bushes by the bottom gate and there were hundreds of other flowers which Charlotte hadn't looked up yet in her Mum's flower book. Overhead a hawk circled lazily.

As Charlotte watched the trees they began to shimmer, or

25

perhaps it was her vision. It looked as if something was coming between her and them. A humming sound started in her ears and she felt as though she was going to pass out. She breathed deeply. She didn't feel afraid, but she did feel very funny. She closed her eyes and tried to make it go away. The buzzing stopped and she felt better. She opened her eyes and nearly fell off the wall.

Everything was different.

There was now a wall going all the way around the trees. Just like her dreams. It was a big one too, about ten or twelve feet high. Down where the path usually came out of the woods there were two immense stone gateposts with an enormous iron gate between them. Charlotte blinked. She looked around cautiously and with a jump she saw that her house was gone. The big chestnut tree stood alone on the hillside. Charlotte wondered immediately and instinctively, whether the wall was designed to keep something in, or to keep things out...

There was nothing in sight. Charlotte looked all the way round her. The cow sheds were gone, and the stream at the bottom of the field was wider and faster, a real river. She looked back to Ken's house and she was surprised to see that it was there, and that she could see more of the chimney, since there were fewer trees blocking the view. The fields looked greener, in fact everything was brighter. The air was still, but the tops of the trees were moving as if there was a breeze. Everything smelt wonderful - just like the inside of the clearing. The elderberry bushes by the wall had both flowers and berries on them at the same time, as if they couldn't decide whether it was spring or autumn.

Charlotte wondered where she was and how she was going to get home. She slid off the low garden wall, although the garden was now gone, and into the field. The grass was thick and deep. Grasshoppers buzzed and butterflies spiralled everywhere. The hawk was still floating overhead. Although the sun was low in the sky the brightness make it seem to be the middle of the afternoon. She began to get a nervous feeling in her stomach. Where was she? What had just happened? She decided to go to Ken's house and see if anyone was there, perhaps she could get help.

She started up the hill. Her driveway was gone, and so were the fence and the wall beside it, and the road and the trees that used to stand by the road. Where the road usually was, there was a vast expanse of downs, grass, short bushes, flowers. No sign that the road had ever existed.

She walked through buttercups and dandelions, milkweed and shepherd's purse. She got a slightly creepy feeling once in a while but all in all it was such a beautiful day that she began to relax; she thought she must be dreaming anyway, although this was like no dream she had ever had. She reached the front gate of the house and peered through the bars. Inside was a beautiful stone house which looked a little bit like Ken's house, as if Ken's house had taken off its clothes – no plaster work or stone columns, the windows and chimney were different – it was smaller too. Sitting outside was an old man smoking a pipe and reading a book. He looked nice enough, and she was trying to decide whether or not to say hello when a dog began to bark.

"STIG!" yelled the old man. "Come on boy, down. Who's out there?" he asked, not sounding too worried.

"Um," said Charlotte, "I'm lost, I'm sorry to startle you." The man reached the gates. He grabbed the dog by the collar and opened them.

"Come on in and tell me where you're from, although," he said squinting at her, "I think I can guess." He walked over to the gates and opened them.

Charlotte stood at the gate, afraid to go inside. "Thanks," she said, and then, "you can?"

"Oh, I think so," he smiled. "But tell me anyway."

"Well, I...' Charlotte didn't know what to say. For one thing, her story sounded strange, but for another, here she was and here HE was living in Ken's house...

Confused, she plunged in. "I was sitting on the wall down there when everything disappeared. I don't know... I mean, my house was just THERE, and then, boom, it wasn't." She stopped.

"You came from Earth didn't you?" he asked, gesturing with his hands on the word 'Earth' as though he was including both her world and his.

"Yes..." said Charlotte, confused.

"Well, this is Earth too, but different. Better. How did you get here?"

"I don't know. There was a humming sound, everything started to shimmer, then I closed my eyes... When I opened them I was here," said Charlotte now more confused at the old man's calmness than anything else.

"Well, I can help you get back. You're not really safe here unless you're practiced at getting home. Did anything strange happen to you on your way here?"

"No," said Charlotte "But I did feel as though something was watching me..."

"Well," said the old man cryptically, "if you're not experienced you risk slipping between the worlds and it's not all as nice as it is here. Well, let's see about sending you home." The dog came up and licked Charlotte's hands.

"Stig likes you. You must be one of us."

Charlotte looked at him curiously. This was all so strange, she was having trouble believing that she was awake.

He regarded her steadily, then nodded to himself as if he'd made some sort of decision. "Well, if you crossed over once, you might cross over again. If you do, and I hope you don't, you should come straight here as fast and as carefully as you can."

He was looking at Charlotte very seriously, and she was beginning to get a little afraid. "You should try to cross back home on your own if you can, but whatever you do, don't be frightened."

"Why – and what do you mean, cross back?" asked Charlotte. The man paused, looked at her and narrowed his eyes slightly. After a silence, he said "Well, don't be frightened because there's nothing to be frightened about and if you're frightened you won't be able to get back to your own home, so easily – that's what it's like, you cross over from there, to here and then back again." He looked at

28

her puzzled face and smiled. " Don't worry. The happier you are, the easier it will be for you to find your way here or to find your way home. You really just have to concentrate very hard on your home and you'll be fine. Just remember not to be frightened, and you'll be OK."

Charlotte got the distinct feeling that he was holding something back, all that rubbish about there being nothing to be frightened of; just what her Mum told her the last time she'd had to have a shot and it still hurt like mad. She may have been only eleven years old, but she wasn't stupid. Never mind. Here she was, probably dreaming, talking to a strange man about strange things... Charlotte guessed that it probably didn't matter what he said to her, she'd still wake up in her own bed. She sighed, and looked at him closely to see if she had made him up out of someone she knew in real life, the way you sometimes do in dreams. He did look slightly familiar, but she couldn't guess who it was he looked like. Well, he was obviously a dream, anyway.

"Come on," said the man, ignoring her look. "I'll send you home." They started off to the gates.

He ushered her outside. As she looked back at him to ask him who he was everything started to shimmer as it had before. "Goodbye, Charlotte," said the man, just before he faded away, and the humming sound started and then died away again in Charlotte's ears.

"Wait!" called Charlotte. "How did you know my name?" But he was already gone.

She was standing by the side of the road right outside Ken's house. The road was just the same as it had always been. She walked up to her own driveway. At the bottom she could see her house. She walked down, and ran into her Mother by the house.

"There you are. You weren't supposed to go very far," she chided Charlotte. "You weren't supposed to go outside at all. Trust your father. Anyway, come in now."

"I just went up the driveway," said Charlotte, not really lying. "Sorry."

"Alright. Well, it's time to come inside now, it's getting

late."

Her mother made her some hot chocolate, and made her go upstairs to bed.

"I'm sorry, you just haven't been working very hard recently, spending all that time in those woods. It's only another four weeks until the holidays," said her mother, tucking her under the covers. "Sometimes I forget we've only just moved here and everything's so new for you. I've gotten so settled in over the past three weeks it feels like home already."

"That's because you and Dad are from here," Charlotte pointed out.

"Well, years ago. I'm sorry. Just keep at the school stuff, it's not much longer, and it will make next year so much easier. Now brush your teeth and get to sleep. You don't have to study until after lunch tomorrow – oh, and your father met Mr. Starling across the way on his walk and arranged for you to go over to see the morning milking if you want, so you have to get up really early if you want to go!" She smiled at Charlotte.

"Cool!" said Charlotte. She ran up, brushed her teeth and hopped into bed. She lay on her back listening to the tree gently brush her window, and she fell asleep and had a perfectly normal dream that a whole herd of cows were in the front yard mooing for her to milk them.

Chapter 3

The next morning Charlotte was awake so early that it was still quite dark. She jumped into her clothes, dying to get to the Starling's farm, see the cows and maybe find out a bit more about the boy who had gone missing and come back. It suddenly struck her that the sun should be up.

'I thought my alarm clock said seven-o-clock,' she thought. She looked again. It was an old fashioned alarm clock with a regular dial and hands that glowed in the dark, and it said quarter to seven. Then as she got closer to the clock she realized it was facing backwards against the mirror on her dressing table, and she had been looking at the reflection. It was only a quarter past five in the morning, but she was wide awake and fully dressed.

She walked over to the window to open the curtains and was over come by a sudden chill and the feeling that if she looked out her front window there would be someone standing under the chestnut tree. She thought maybe she'd feel better if she was warmer so she went and put on a jumper.

While she was putting it on she started thinking about seeing the cows. Maybe, she thought, the farmer would teach her how to milk a cow. Maybe she could get a cow of her own and learn how to make butter and cheese. She started to feel better. She walked over to the window and reached out towards the curtain. She paused for a second. 'Silly,' she told herself, 'being afraid of the dark,' and she threw open the curtain. Her heart beat madly, and her vision began to fade. She could hear the low, watery buzzing sound in her ears and she shut her eyes and tried not to pass out. When she opened them, she could see that the green girl was standing under the tree below her window, but behind her something was coming, something dark and fast and terrifying. Charlotte let out a yell, and then her vision clouded over.

A little after six, her mother shook her awake. "Come on, wake up, you're going to miss the cows." Charlotte didn't care about the cows anymore, she just wanted to sleep. Her mother shook her again. "What are you doing asleep on the windowsill with your clothes on? Toast's on, come and get it before it's cold."

Two pieces of toast and some orange juice later, Charlotte, her dad and the dog were heading down the field and over to the cow sheds. "We've got some time," said her dad. "Farmer Starling gets up before six to start the milking, and they've got over a hundred cows to milk, it takes until seven thirty to finish."

"How do they milk so many cows? Are there milkmaids? Can I learn how to be one?"

"No," said her dad, smiling, "they've got a machine that does it all."

"Really? How?"

"Well, it's got a hose with four rubber cups on the end of it. Each cup fits over one of the cow's teats and then the machine gently sucks the milk out, like a calf, and pumps it into a tank. Something like that. It does ten at a time."

"Wow."

They were at the bottom of the field, quite close to the wood. The grass was wet with dew, and the ground by the small stream was muddy. There were small, cloven hoof prints around the edge.

"Deer," said Mr. Enright. "You can tell, they're too small to be cows and there's no sheep in this field. They probably live in the woods. They get out the same way you get in, through that gap in the hedge. Probably if there were farm animals in this field the farmer would mend that gap."

They crossed the plank over the stream, dragged Roger away from the deer prints and climbed the stile into the bottom field on the other side. The barns were just at the top, about a ten minute climb. When they got into the upper field, Charlotte turned and looked back at her house. She could see the whole front of the house from where she was, and to the left she could see the woods. They looked alive. The trees all moved in time with the wind, first one way, and then another. She saw one patch of trees moving in a different direction from the rest of the woods for a while, which was

32

strange, but it must be the wind. "They're beautiful," she thought, then turned around.

The farm was built on the other side of the hill, with the sheds on the top. The woods curved up the slope opposite Charlotte's house, over the hill, down again towards the Starling's farm quite close, about thirty feet from the rear of the house. The woods carried down the hill to the bottom, and over a small river.

There was a cluster of cows by the open door of the first shed, and a few more grazing around them. When they got closer Charlotte and her father could see that the cluster of cows was actually inside a small pen around a door into the barn. As they watched, another door opened beside the pen and one, two... five... eightnineten cows hurried out followed by a young man waving a stick and yelling "Yah... yah... gurron with it... yah!" A rail lifted at the door and ten cows filed through one at a time before the bar fell down. No one was shooing them in. Charlotte wanted to know why.

"Well," said Mr. Enright, "they want to be milked. Their udders get painful with too much milk and no calf to suckle. Besides, there's food in the barn!"

"Where're the calves?"

"They get sold at market..."

Charlotte didn't like to think about the calves.

"Some of them get to stay and become milk cows too," her father added. "Good," said Charlotte.

The farmer caught sight of them through the door and ushered them in. When they arrived he was busy hooking cows up to the machine and patting each one on the head. "Got to spend a moment with each one. They like attention, do cows."

"Thanks for letting us come, this is Charlotte, my daughter," said Mr. Enright.

"Hullo there. Ever seen cows this close before?"

"No," admitted Charlotte, feeling a little shy.

"Big, in't they!" he laughed.

The dairy smelt sweet and fresh, warm milk and hay and cows. The floor was concrete and got hosed down to keep the place clean, so there was no bad smell, or mud underfoot. Sparkling clean. Ted Starling's two sons, Ted and James were busy around the sheds. Charlotte wondered which one had gone missing.

Farmer "Call me Big Ted" Starling was a pleasant man. He was fiftyish and lean, really wiry and strong. His face was slightly red from the work and the sun. He was a little shorter than Charlotte's dad, but he seemed bigger. He had a receding hairline, but his hair was still quite brown, and he had a few ragged whiskers testifying to the fact that he hadn't shaved yet that morning. His oldest son, Ted (18 and called "young Ted"), was busy helping him, by shooing out the cows.

James, the youngest at 16 was meandering around picking things up. He showed them the feed room and inside the milk tank where a big blade slowly moved the milk around. "I'm not usually in 'ere in the mornings," he said, "but this morning I woke up at five o clock and couldn't get back to sleep, so I went out and did some work. Checked on the sheep, kicked the chickens out of bed early and came over to help out here."

Big Ted called over to Charlotte. "Want to touch a cow?" he asked. Charlotte walked over and looked, he motioned to her to go on. The cow smelt nice, a mustier version of the smell of the barn. Charlotte reached out and touched the cow's udder. It was really warm and soft, fuzzy. The cow twitched an ear and raised a hind hoof to warn her. She looked at the cow. It looked back. It looked friendly. She reached a hand up and the cow swung her big head slowly towards it, sniffed it, decided that Charlotte wasn't offering any food, and swung her head back to the feed tray.

She decided to memorize the cow's markings so could recognize her in the field. The cow was white with dark brown spots (a Friesian, according to Big Ted). She looked just like all the other cows.

Charlotte stepped back and looked carefully at all the spots. There were five on the cow's left side, she memorized their pattern. There was one on the cow's rear flank that looked a bit like a cat. She thought she could tell the animal apart from the others, but she didn't know for sure.

"Do you give your cows names?" she asked. "How do you tell them apart?"

"See this?" asked Big Ted, pointing to a tag in the cow's ear. The earring had the number 211 on it. "I've got a list in the back with all the numbers on it next to names, vet reports, so on. There's so many cows that some of 'em even have the same names. I can remember most of them. I think this one's... no, I'll look it up for you. I can see you've taken a shine to her."

There was plenty of time before the end of the milking for Charlotte to look around. She watched young Ted work, letting the cows out of their stalls and into a walkway that went to the barn door. She watched the machine pull milk out of the cows, and looked at the tank where it ended up. "Don't get Dad on about his cows," said James, standing beside her. "He loves his cows, does Dad. Me too, really."

After, while James hosed down the shed, they went into the back and Big Ted looked up cow number 211. "Bluebell," he said. "I thought so. This one was born over in those woods by your house. Her mother was an escape artist. Climbed walls and everything. How she managed to get into that wood when she was ready to drop, I'll never know. We found her happy as a clown in the middle of all those bluebells one morning with this one tottering around like a drunk. We had to carry the calf back up the hill with her mother mooing behind her."

"And you cussing all the way," said Ted Jr. The story had obviously been told before, all three of the Starlings were laughing to themselves.

"I thought you were going to start blowing steam out of your ears," said James.

"Strangest thing though, cows normally don't bother going in the woods. No food, you see," said Big Ted.

Charlotte thought about the strange coincidences. Firstly James being woken up at the same time as her this morning, and secondly the cow that she picked out from the herd being born in the woods.

She went over to James and asked him why he was up so early.

"Probably the woods," he said. Charlotte jumped. "What?"

"Those woods, they sound like voices talking from far away. Sometimes they sound like a river, or maybe the sea."

"Can you hear them from here?"

"You know down this hill where they start?"

"Yes?"

"Well, that little valley goes around the corner just out of sight and they curve around to just behind our house. I can hear them from my bedroom window. They keep me awake some nights. Sometimes on a still night I can hear the woods moving, they rustle as if some breeze was blowing. I keep thinking I'm hearing someone outside and I can't sleep."

"I woke up last night a bit before five, thought I saw someone outside," said Charlotte.

"Funny," continued James "I woke up a bit before five this morning too. I was looking out the window and suddenly thought I saw this man outside, I went out to see him but 'e was gone."

"Who was it?"

"Well, I don't know," said James, looking at his feet. "I used to 'ave these dreams when I were younger, like your age. I thought 'e was real. I used to dream we'd go all through the woods and 'e'd show me things like my Granddad. He taught me how to make a straight bow and arrow, how to fish in the pool down the hill, all sorts of things. He were just made up though... I mean, 'e was green, not bright like a Martian or anything, but, sort of woody, mossy. Loads of people have seen things in these woods, loads, not just me." He looked up at Charlotte and chuckled. "Anyway, I thought I'd seen 'im this morning, but probably another dream. 'Aven't thought about it for ages either. If you've seen 'im; you're dreaming too, that's all I have to say," he laughed.

"I'm surprised you still go in those woods James," interrupted young Ted, "it's dangerous in there, you should know that."

"Why?" asked Charlotte.

"Well," said James "Ted believes all these old st..."

"James!" exclaimed Ted "don't talk rubbish. They're NOT old stories, it's happened twice in the last ten years."

"Ted..." warned James.

"What's happened?" Charlotte wanted to know "Is it really dangerous in the woods?" Her father was listening in.

"There's been a few funny goings on in there, like people, youngsters, going missing. James here went missing himself when he was younger. We found him wandering around in a daze claiming men had "'taken him away'" and he says he's never been able to remember anything."

"That's not all true!" James retorted. "I just went for a walk and got lost."

"For a week?"

"I don't know, I can't remember..."

"See?" said Ted "He's nuts. He loves those woods. Him and that mad Ken Stone."

"We're not mad. Don't pick on Ken, he's just young."

"Listen to you. Only two and half years older and calling Ken young! Anyway, Ken is strange at that."

Charlotte interrupted them. "I've met Ken in the woods, he knows his way around just fine."

"You've been going into the woods?" asked young Ted, concerned.

"Yes, it's beautiful and peaceful in there. Besides, I've got Roger. Where is Roger?" she asked.

"Out back with Ted and Bo."

"Ted and Bo? There's another Ted?" asked Charlotte's dad who'd been quietly listening to the conversation.

"Yeah," chuckled James. "The dogs. Young Ted spent a summer over at an uncle's farm a couple of years ago and got the dog. For a laugh he called it Ted Three and by the time he got it home two months later it was too late, it already answered to Ted..." Both the boys were chuckling to themselves. "Drives Dad mad!" explained James.

Charlotte was listening to the boys talk. Their voices were

soft and rumbly. They both had a strong accent and sometimes it was hard to follow what they said. Just then the dogs came careening around the corner, Roger leading. "Get those blooming dogs out of here!" yelled Old Ted. "That's your mutt there Ted, I saw that."

"Sorry Dad," they chorused back.

"This sounds dangerous," said Mr. Enright after a pause. "Charlotte, maybe you shouldn't go into those woods so much."

"Oh, Dad..." Charlotte wailed. "It's beautiful in there. If anything was going to happen, it would have already."

Her father opened his mouth to argue, but before he could say anything, Big Ted, who was still standing with them piped up, "James is right," he said, "there's nothing to worry about in there. Only people missing in there are just lost. I've lived next to these woods all my life and there's nothing there that's not good and peaceful. I don't know, it all seems like old wives tales to me. Keep an eye open, if you like, but don't worry, it's just fine in there."

Mr. Enright seemed mollified a little. "Just take Roger with you all the time," he said. "It's time for us to go now."

"Here," said Big Ted picking up a basket of eggs from the floor beside him. "You can run the basket back over with this 'un," he waved in Charlotte's direction. "I can see 'er and James have lots in common. Let 'im take her around, 'e knows what's what. You sure you can't stay for something to eat?"

"Thanks so much for the eggs and the offer," said Mr. Enright, "but my wife's expecting us back. By the way, I almost forgot. Mary wants to raise some chickens. I thought you may be able to give her a few pointers."

"Just tell her to give us a ring when she's ready. She can come over and help Carol with the hens and stay for tea. We can get you some pullets much cheaper than from the market."

"That's wonderful. You must let us do something for you... I'll tell Mary to call. Thanks for spending so much time with us..."

"Thanks a lot," added Charlotte, taking the hint.

"Don't think about it," said Big Ted. He and his sons waved them off. They started walking across the field. About twenty feet from the farm, Charlotte was knocked off her balance by Roger, who came bowling in from behind them, followed by Ted Three and Bo. Mr. Enright turned around to look at the dogs. "Go on home!" he said. The two Starling dogs ran furiously in a circle around them before racing back to the farm. "Dogs!"

They walked down the field, back across the stream and started up the other side. Charlotte was in a good mood. She yelled "Hey!" and heard *ey... y* in return.

"Yaaaahhh" yelled her Dad. They heard *aaa... aa... a*

"Three echoes. I only got two," said Charlotte.

"Well, I'm way bigger than you."

"So," she taunted, "I could still race you to the garden wall and win."

"Well you just try it!"

"ReadysteadyGO!" she yelled, taking off running up the hill.

Her Dad started running up the hill behind her. "Not fair! You started before the GO!"

At the wall, it was a tied race, Charlotte's Dad puffing his way behind her and just catching up at the very end, clutching the egg basket carefully.

"About time too," said Mrs. Enright. "What took you so long? Roger's been home long enough to eat half his bowl already! Here, I've made pancakes, have some breakfast."

After breakfast Charlotte was tired enough for a nap. She lay in bed, wondering what had really happened to James and if she had just dreamed the Green King as well. She really wanted to go back and meet James again to ask him more questions, but before she could think what to ask, she fell asleep to a dream that she was in the clearing with a horde of people, some green, some normal looking, all dancing around to music, eating, drinking strange drinks and talking at once. Charlotte was one of them, in this bizarre little dream, and she knew exactly what was going on.

She was sitting on a rock inside the clearing. Roger was there, bounding around in the trees, going up to everyone he saw and licking their hands or their faces. She looked at her hands, and they were green, too. In fact, she was green all over, and she was wearing clothing made from what looked like leaves sewn together, or spun into cloth. Soft clothes, not prickly at all. People were coming up and hugging her, Someone gave her a piece of fruit that she didn't quite recognize, but it tasted good when she bit into it.

The trees around the clearing were moving, but not in the breeze. They were reaching branches over to each other, waving them around, rustling leaves... *talking* Charlotte realized. She could see plumes of smoke coming up from small stone structures in the ground, and a few people walking around. There were lights in the branches of the trees, the clearing was obviously the central meeting place. She felt great, as if she'd finally come home. She heard a small voice.

A girl – the same one she had seen before – took her hand and led her out of the clearing and along the path she always took. She and her companion, who was her own age and who said she was called Gaua, walked right to the edge of the woods. The gap in the woods that Charlotte used to get in was now the gates she had seen when she had met the old man in Ken's house.

Gaua said that the wall circled the whole wood, and that there were gates at four points - her gap, Ken's gap, a path she hadn't seen but which James used, and the bridge into town. Gaua also told her that the woods were magical, and that there were three points of power in the woods. The chestnut trees in the clearing were one point and they were the first chestnut trees, the oldest trees in the woods.

The clearing was the centre of the woods, the meeting place, the safest place. The other points were a ruined house, and a big tree, now a dead, hollow stump. Charlotte recognized it as the mound she had seen the afternoon when she had picked the bluebells.

The ruins held the guardian of the woods, although what or

who that was wasn't clear. The stump was a dark, brooding place, with its own watchman, its own laws; an uncertain and dark place. A gateway. A dangerous place for the careless.

Gaua led her back to the houses, which were the stone buildings Charlotte had seen near the clearing. Dug into the ground with only the roofs showing, they seemed lovely and cosy. Scattered through the green woods were fruit trees, and small patches of garden. There were birds running around - quails, kept instead of chickens. For an instant Charlotte glimpsed the old Green King through the trees, the same man she had seen before. It was a beautiful place. Gaua took both of Charlotte's hands, smiled into her eyes and bid her goodbye. Just as she was waking up, she heard Gaua tell her not to worry about the dog, that a friend would bring him back.

Charlotte felt a heaviness around her legs and woke up out of the dream. The first thing she did was look around her room for Roger. Sometimes when she was sleeping, the dog would creep in and sleep on the rug beside her bed. He wasn't there, so she figured he was with her parents. She looked out of her window. Under the tree she could see the deck chairs where they were lying. Her mother was reading, her father was asleep. She put on her clothes and went downstairs. Roger was nowhere in the house, so she went out to her parents.

"Where's Roger?" she asked her mother quietly, so as not to disturb her sleeping father.

"Oh my goodness, the dog. I've been dozing for a while, I just woke up. I never even thought about him. He's probably wandered off somewhere. Still, let's have a look for him, shall we?" She put down her book with a sigh and got up.

Charlotte was thinking. Gaua had told her in her dream not to worry about the dog. Was this the sort of dream that James had had when he was her age? Was it because she'd talked to James that she'd had the dream?

Her mother had gotten up and was walking around to the back of the house, calling for Roger. Charlotte followed her.

41

They continued walking, and were back in front of the house and headed to the bottom of the garden to see if the dog was in the field when they saw Ken Stone coming out of the gap in the hedge, followed by Roger.

Ken walked up. "Found yer dog in the bushes. He dived out of nowhere, landed right on me. Blighter. You ought to keep 'un tied up. If one of the farmers catches him with sheep they'll shoot him even if he's not doing anything. There's enough dogs wandering around savaging sheep that they don't even think. If it's not their dog, farmers'll shoot it."

Charlotte was on her knees by the dog scolding him. "Don't ever do that again. You hear?" Roger slathered her hands with his tongue, and sat in front of her panting and dragging his tail back and forth over the grass. "Oh, you..." she was laughing, relieved to have the dog back.

"Want to go for a walk?" asked Ken

"Sure," Charlotte replied. "Can I go for a walk with Ken?" she asked her mother, who was watching her with amusement.

"Alright, just take your watch and be back by lunch. It's ten now, be back by noon."

Charlotte raced inside and up to her room to get her watch. It was sitting on her dresser, and beside it was a leaf. She looked at the leaf and thought it must have come out of her hair from when she fell. There were others on the floor by the window. She shrugged to herself, used now to leaves appearing in her room at strange times – maybe the window blew open sometimes? She went downstairs, putting on the watch as she went. She and Ken set off across the field below the house to the woods.

"Have you seen that old house in there?" asked Ken. "No," she said.

"It's just the walls, but I like to sit in there and do stuff sometimes."

"What sort of stuff?"

"Oh, anything. Sometimes I carve bits of wood, I don't know. I like it in there. It used to be a gamekeeper's hut, I think. There's a big house across the woods from us, and it used to be a manor house. Our house and your house used to be labourer's cottages, I think your house used to be two, ours used to be three, all rolled in together. That's why the houses are so big."

"Our house isn't that big," said Charlotte "It's only got three bedrooms."

"Well, they weren't big cottages. Ours was added on to since it was built. Well, anyway, this place is quite old. There was a fire or something and now it's just walls."

"We walked past it that once and I've always meant to go in there and look. I usually end up in the clearing down that way," and she pointed over, deeper into the woods and down the slope. From the corner of her eye she thought she could see something moving. She looked up but it disappeared. Ken was talking.

"That's where you saw the deer, yes?"

"Yup."

"He's a hard one to see. I saw him for the first time years ago, then I didn't see him for a long time and I thought he was dead. I saw him again, about a year and a half ago. I've only seen him three times, last time was just before you moved in."

"Well, he must be in the woods around here now, I've seen him three times in the last two weeks. It was the same one, I'm sure. Really big antlers, too many tines to count." Charlotte looked sideways at Ken to see if he had noticed that she had used the correct word. No response. Typical. She went on.

"He's much bigger than the others I've seen, and he's greyer, too. I saw him really close in the clearing, but he ran away so fast I didn't even see him move, he just disappeared into the bushes."

"Three times?" Ken was surprised, then thoughtful. He looked at her and looked down again, drew in a breath and decided to tell her what he was thinking. "He's not a normal deer, you know."

"What do you mean?" Charlotte didn't know whether to

43

laugh or be frightened.

"The first time I saw him was about four years ago. I was in the woods with my dog..."

"I didn't know you had a dog?" interrupted Charlotte.

"He's dead, now."

"Sorry. Umm, how, I mean...?"

"Well, it's all part of the same story."

Charlotte listened closer to Ken as they walked. "I was in the woods with Stig..." Charlotte jumped and breathed in sharply. "My dog," he explained with a curious look at her, "and I heard this music, or wind, or something. Over by the clearing. Stig heard the noise and raced over to it. I couldn't stop him or anything, he was barking and wagging his tail like he knew what was going on. I followed him, and I saw that boy James from the farm across the way."

"James Starling?" Charlotte had an idea what was coming next.

"Yes. How did you know?"

"I met him this morning. He likes the woods a lot, too. Something strange... I don't know." Charlotte was thinking about the remarks that James and young Ted had said about the woods. People missing. James gone for a week. Strange men 'taking him away', the thoughts all moved around in her head in a cloud. She was beginning to make some sort of connection, something about the woods, something about James and Ken, something about her dreams... but she couldn't quite grasp it. Ken was still talking.

"...over in the clearing with flowers all over him," (Charlotte guessed he was talking about James) "and these people. Green people with leaves all over them, lots of them prancing about and this one man, really old, and they were all laughing, then Stig ran right into the middle of it, and I swear, I swear all these people froze and started to look like DEER! This old man turned right into that old grey stag, and then BOOM, they were gone. All except old James, he fell down crying, yelling and all that, I don't know. Anyway, I beat it out of there. But Stig wouldn't come. He was in the clearing, whining. He started howling and howling and then,

44

BOOM, he disappeared too. Wandered into some tree roots and never came out. No tunnel, nothing. Found his collar stuck to a twig. No one believes me, though, 'cept maybe my Mum knows something, she's not telling. Everyone just thinks he ran away. I was only nine or ten. I got home and told Mum, and she called people and they went in and got James. 'Parently he'd been gone for a week. Nobody told me."

"The Green King???" Charlotte queried in amazement.

"Oh, alright then, don't believe me," sighed Ken.

"No, that's not... but..." she spluttered, but he was walking faster down the path, away from her.

Charlotte was riveted to the spot. What was going on? What was in these woods? Why was she seeing things?

Once again she got the feeling she was being watched. Ken was walking ahead of her silently along the thin rabbit-way in the underbrush. She looked around, not afraid, but extremely curious. Ever since that morning, the corners of her eyes were full of moving things. When she looked right at them there was always nothing there, but if she looked straight ahead of her she could definitely see things at the edge of her vision. Figures, moving. One figure taking shape. Her ears filled with the same liquid, vibrant humming sound, that gradually got louder and louder.

She almost looked but kept her head down. "Just keep my eyes on the path," she thought, "and only look out of the corners..." It seemed to be working. She was beginning to see a definite figure keeping pace with herself and Ken. It was the Green King, she was certain.

As they walked, she started moving her head ever so slowly from where it was and looking towards the figure. Two things happened at once. Ken stopped and said "Here!" and she finished her slow turn and raised her eyes sharply to look right into the face of the old Green King. She started, and uttered an involuntary sound, just a little, 'ah'. The man disappeared. Ken saw the deer for a second and yelled "Hey! That's him!" Tendrils of darkness reached for her from out of nowhere, and then blackness closed over everything.

Charlotte thought she could hear laughter and it made the darkness fade a little. For a moment, the laughter and the darkness seemed to battle each other, and then she passed out.

Chapter 4

Charlotte was grounded for the week that followed because her parents were worried about her health since she passed out in the woods. She had been to the doctor, who made her take loads of blood tests, prodded her, took her blood pressure and eventually said that she was alright. She still wasn't supposed to go anywhere by herself outside except the garden, not even the clearing.

At school she moaned to Rosemary, and they made plans for Rosemary to come over to Charlotte's house for dinner on Friday night.

On Thursday evening Charlotte had some sewing to do for class which she took to her bedroom. She put the cushions on the windowsill that overlooked the side of the house, turned on her radio and sat and sewed in the window.

She could smell supper being cooked downstairs. Outside she could hear her father coming home. Roger was rolling in something out in the yard. There was a light breeze and she could hear the chestnut tree in front of the house brushing against the window; a light hissing sound as the tips of the leaves touched glass.

She looked out of her window a while and could see the higher part of the woods. It was a part she never usually went into, as the clearing was further down the hill. There was a gap in the fencing that Ken used to get into 'his' part of the woods, and the ruined house was in this high part.

The ruins were nice inside. After she had woken up from her faint she had gone inside with Ken to recover before walking home. It was quiet and dim, the shadows getting thick on the pathway. There were different trees, more oaks and beeches and they grew taller and closer together than the chestnuts further down in the valley. Funnily enough, inside the ruins the air smelt a lot like it did inside the clearing. Sweeter, warmer, something very different.

"Ouch!!"

Charlotte had accidentally pricked her finger. She started concentrating on her sewing homework. Fifteen minutes

47

later she was finished. She looked up from where she had been sitting and breathed a deep sigh of accomplishment. She got off the sill and stretched, and leaned on it, looking over at the woods. She sometimes saw the deer grazing in the field by the trees, and she knew they liked to come out in the evening. There weren't any to be seen, so she went down to see if she could beg a biscuit.

The next day was Friday, the day of Rosemary's visit. Charlotte met her outside after classes.

"D'you want to go right home, or do you want to walk around a bit?" asked Rosemary.

"I don't know," Charlotte replied. She rather fancied the idea of walking around, but knew her mother would be waiting for them. Still, she sometimes took a later bus home, and it would be alright if they were only a little late.

The two girls walked along, Rosemary pointing things out.

"And that's the house me Gran used to live in before she died. She was born in this town, over the other side, by the edge of the woods."

"Do they have a name, those woods?" Charlotte wondered. She hadn't ever thought before that they may have a name.

"They're called Porter's Forest after the old manor house up there, that's what Gran said anyway, but everyone just calls them 'the woods', really. I mean, they are the only ones.

"My street's called Porter's road, too," said Charlotte excitedly.

"The Porters owned most of this town once," said Rosemary "there's a Porter's Street, Porter's Crescent, the elementary school is called the Edward Porter Elementary, and the library named after them, too. There's a museum actually inside the Manor house, on the other side of the woods from you, same side that I was born on, I was born on Porter's Crescent. It's a bit much, really..."

Charlotte agreed. She marvelled at how everyone she met, and everything she did seemed to bring her back to the woods. Why was it so important to everybody what went on in there? Why was Ken so fascinated with them? Most of all, she wondered if there really was someone living in the woods, and if so, who was it, or rather, what was it? Something mysterious was definitely happening.

Charlotte hesitated to ask Rosemary, but she really wanted to know more about the woods.

"What is it with those trees? Why is everyone so interested in them? What's all this about a man living in there? You said you saw him once...

They walked a little further in silence, Rosemary not saying anything.

There were quite a few people out on the old streets. The narrow ways between the buildings rang with cars and people going home, children yelling at each other, dogs barking. It was quite sunny outside, it still felt like early afternoon. Rosemary was walking along thinking seriously. She stared at her feet, her dark brown hair catching the sun as it bounced with her footsteps. Her school clothes were wrinkled, her trousers a bit dusty on the knees. Rosemary liked to run around a lot with her bunch of friends during lunch, they were always being caught outside the school limits, or inside, scurrying around the classrooms. She looked over at Charlotte and smiled.

"Race you to the sweet shop!"

The sweet shop was around the corner and was a favourite hangout after classes. There was always a line-up at the counter of people buying sweets and gum. The two girls pulled into the store breathlessly giggling. Inside was a large group of kids including Tony Harbrook, a boy two years ahead of them. He was with his older brother, who was flirting with the girl behind the counter. They saw the girls walk in, and Tony waved. To Charlotte's surprise, Rosemary was beginning to blush, although it was difficult to tell beneath her dark skin. She was smiling and saying something to Tony, being very coy. After the boys left, Charlotte challenged Rosemary: "You've got a crush on Tony Harbrook."

49

"Do not!" said Rosemary, going so red that it was obvious.

"Do too, you like him. I saw you. You're blushing. And he's too old. He'll be in fourth year next year..."

"Third," interrupted Rosemary.

"...and you'll only be in second," finished Charlotte.

"Shhh!" hissed Rosemary, even though no one could hear them. "Anyway," she added, "me Dad's five years older than me Mum." They reached the counter.

"Four Mojos," asked Charlotte, holding out her coins.

"One liquorice wheel," said Rosemary, holding it for the girl to see and paying for it. The girl behind the counter was smiling at Rosemary with a knowing look on her face. She had already finished school and was dating Tony's older brother, Simon. Rosemary was blushing really badly still.

As they left the store Charlotte started laughing. Just then, the two boys came out of the shop on the corner. The boys saw them, and while Simon walked ahead, Tony slowed down to talk to Rosemary.

"Simon's got his car with him. Do you want a ride home?"

"Yes," said Rosemary jumping at the offer, and then, "Oh, I'm going to Charlotte's house for tea, it's the other way."

"I'll ask Simon," he said, and then yelled to his brother. Simon slowed down. "Can we drive Rosemary and her friend over to... where is it...?"

"Porter's road," said Charlotte.

"...Porter's road?" finished Tony.

"It's alright, we're almost at the bus stop..." began Charlotte, but then Rosemary turned and glared so hard at her that she finished with, "but we're late, it would be nice..." She looked back at Rosemary who was still glaring at her.

"'S not too bad," said Simon. "Just take five minutes."

Charlotte wasn't too sure what her Mum and Dad would think about her riding home in a strange car, but she couldn't see how they'd object. Rosemary was chatting along happily.

They got into the car, a small Morris Minor, ancient and hiccuppy. With Tony and Rosemary in the back, Charlotte was forced to sit up front with the older boy, who was obviously not interested in anything except getting them home as fast as possible.

In the back seat Rosemary and Tony were giggling over something. Charlotte could hardly hear them over the noise of the old engine; honestly it was actually worse than her Dad's car. They were just started on the road to Charlotte's house, and there wasn't very far to go.

"Thanks for the ride, Simon," said Charlotte.

"'S OK," he answered. "'S on the way to Ted's place, I 'aven't seen the Starlings for a while, think we'll drop in on 'em."

"You know the Starlings?" piped up Charlotte.

"Yeah. Young Ted and I were in school together, and James is a year ahead of Tony. 'E's a strange one. I remember when 'e was eleven 'e went missing, for a whole week. You should have seen the town. Everyone was crazy, boy gone missing and all that. Me and me Dad went out with the Teds looking for them. Tons of people went looking."

"I remember that!" interrupted Rosemary. "We was living with me Gran by the woods, and she told us we couldn't ever go in there again. She said the fairies had gotten him or some rubbish."

"Isn't there supposed to be some ghost living in there?" Tony asked. Rosemary laughed. "Funny you should ask that, Charlotte was just asking me that before we saw you."

"Well?" chorused Charlotte and Tony, and then Tony said "Snap!" at the same time as Charlotte said "Jinx". They looked at each other and laughed again. Some sort of tension had been broken, and Rosemary shrugged and launched into her story.

"Me Gran always said that the little people lived in the trees. Fairies, Pixies, Leprauchauns, I don't know. She knew all these old stories. She said that when she was young, a little girl and several babies went missing. She said that everybody knew it was these fairies, they all believed in them. The police were looking for a man they said was living in there, but everyone thought it was the king of the

51

fairies or some nonsense." Her audience was quiet.

"When I was about eight I saw this man in there, looked like a tree stump or something. Scared me, I can tell you. Me Gran told me I had seen the King, and that I should never go back into the woods because he would take me and I'd never get out. She said you could only see him if he let you, and he only let you if he was going to take you. I was so scared. I haven't been back in there since."

"Is he a bad man?" wondered Charlotte.

"Course," shrugged Tony.

"No," said Rosemary. "Me Gran said he was King of the beautiful people. That's what she called them, I remember. The Beautiful people, the fairies. They're supposed to be good but they need human babies to breed with because they're dying out. Still sounds like rubbish to me."

"But, I mean..." Charlotte was fumbling for a way to say what she was thinking. Tony butted in and said it for her:

"People and Fairies can't have babies together. If there are fairies. It'd be like trying to breed cats and dogs. Can't do it."

"Me Gran said they're just like us," said Rosemary, a little petulantly. "You two don't have to believe me, I don't care if there are fairies or not, that's just what me Gran said, and YOU asked me, so shut up."

"Sorry Rosemary," Charlotte apologised, and then they were at Charlotte's driveway.

The rest of the evening passed quickly and Rosemary and Charlotte explored the old barns for an hour after tea before Mr. Enright drove her home.

They had found nothing of interest, but played a game of ghost in which Rosemary scared Charlotte silly by pretending to be the ghost of the barn, which involved hiding in the rafters making noises. They had become fast friends, especially since Charlotte knew Rosemary's secret about Tony. Rosemary teased her about Ken, but agreed he was cute, so they made a pact to keep each other's secrets and to help each other out.

After Rosemary left, Charlotte went to her bedroom and sat

in the side window looking out over the fields in the late evening light.

Outside, the sun was just on the horizon and the woods cast a dark silhouette across the field. The shadows were coming on so quickly that Charlotte caught sight of Ken's shadow long before she actually spotted him running like the wind, not looking behind him, not really looking in front of him. As he got closer to the edge of the Enright's small field Charlotte realized he wasn't just running because he was late, he was running blindly away from something.

She looked beyond Ken but couldn't see a thing. She glanced at the woods curiously, but at first she saw nothing. As she stared at the trees she noticed the tops moving back and forth as if in a tremendous breeze. She watched longer and noticed that the branches weren't all moving in the same direction. Some of the trees were circling one way, other groups were moving in the opposite direction, and some were just flailing back and forth.

She then noticed that the grass was still. Bushes along the edge of the field were still. The only things moving were Ken and the trees. Ken had rounded the end of the field, hopped the fence and was almost at the top of the hill going up to his house. He left her sight, and she continued watching the trees, spellbound.

The sun was doing its last dive below the hill, setting the clouds at the top of the hills alive with colour. Twilight had already fallen at the bottom of the slope. At the top the trees had slowed their wild motion.

Suddenly the trees moved in one slow spiral, which ended at the mouth of the pathway. A bubble of sickly green fog blew out of the trees, expanding so fast it was almost too fast to see. Just as soon as it had started, it was gone. In the dark evening, nothing moved.

She wondered if anyone else had seen what she had just witnessed. Her parents were downstairs and couldn't see over the garden wall. No one else had a view of that field. Ken's house was surrounded by trees so she thought that unless he had stopped to watch and was braver than she

53

would have ever believed, that he would have seen nothing.

She got off the window and went downstairs, but even if she'd been looking carefully, in the dying light she still would have missed the figure that crept out of the woods. A human, an older boy. James Starling, perhaps?

Chapter 5

Mrs. Enright woke Charlotte up at nine-thirty with cinnamon toast and juice.

"Here you go, breakfast in bed and a sleep in."

"Whoa! Great, why?" asked Charlotte.

"Well, I just felt like it. I phoned Carol Starling and we're going over in a while for tea and a lesson in keeping chickens."

"Can I take Roger for a walk later?"

"Only if someone goes with you."

"But it's been a week already, can't I go?"

"No", said Charlotte's mother. "James has offered to take you walking this afternoon. He usually takes their dogs for a ramble if they aren't working with the sheep."

"Thanks anyway, Mum," slumped Charlotte, munching toast. "Better than nothing."

"Well, I want to take a look around in there too, I haven't had much of a chance at all recently, maybe I'll come with you."

"Um... if you want," said Charlotte reluctantly.

"What, you don't want me to come along?"

"It's not that," said Charlotte "I don't really mind at all. I'd rather be in there on my own anyway, so if I'm already going with James, it's okay if you come too."

"Gee thanks," said her mother, mock frowning.

"Oh Mum..." Charlotte started to launch into explanations when she saw her mother smiling at her. She smiled back, shook her head, and started munching at her toast. She was in quite good spirits, with only a week to go in school.

Carol Starling was a plump and pink woman who managed to keep her three men under iron control. She took Charlotte and Mrs. Enright to the chicken shed and showed them how to pick up a bird and check for mites, what sort of places to look for eggs if they suspected a bird was laying somewhere other than the shed.

They could feed the birds table scraps, all cooked up and mashed, along with chicken feed, and some sea-shells to help make the egg shells hard. The Starlings had a bag of oyster shells they'd picked up on the beach, and they smashed them up for the hens. Mrs. Starling mentioned that bags of gravel and shells were for sale in town in case they didn't have time to get their own shells. Without the extra calcium from the shells, the chickens would lay eggs with really thin shells that broke easily.

"Young Ted goes and gets them for us. He loves the sea 'bout as much as James loves those woods. Anyway, if you get a hen laying outside, she may be going broody, and be hiding eggs somewhere and sitting on them. A broody hen is one that wants to hatch her eggs." She added to Charlotte, who was totally baffled, and wondering if this was the 'birds' part of the 'birds and the bees' chat her father was always going on about having one day.

"If you like and you have a rooster, chances are the eggs are fertilized and she may even hatch a few chicks. Best thing if you want chicks is to wait until a hen goes broody, lock her in her own pen and collect really fresh laid eggs, still warm, and start putting them under her. Eight or ten is probably good. If you let her sit on her own outside, half of them'll probably be bad, these hens are used to being fed at the same time every night, so they get off their eggs and go eat, then the eggs go cold."

Mrs. Starling and Charlotte's mother went inside to make tea, and Charlotte wandered around the farm for a while, looking into barns and petting the dogs. She could hear a stream. 'That must be the start of the river James mentioned,' thought Charlotte. She meandered back to the house and went into the kitchen to have some tea with the older women.

Inside, James was there, washing his hands and talking to Mrs. Enright. "We'll just go down to the bottom of the woods where it goes into the town," he was saying. "It's about fifteen or twenty minutes walk to the other side, quite nice, really. You can cross into town if you like, but you have to walk further to the bridge. There's a river beside the wood, quite a big one, fed by all the streams in the area. I fish there sometimes."

"Are we going for a walk?" piped up Charlotte.

At the sound of those magic words Roger, who was hiding under the table waiting for handouts, blundered out and stood up tongue lolling out, ears pointed up and tail waving wildly.

"Well, we have to now, don't we?" said Mrs. Enright.

After they had washed up their cups they all started off across the fields with the dogs running boisterously around them. James was doing most of the talking.

"The woods are so beautiful. I've been in lots of woods, but these ones seem different. They're older, for one thing. These trees have been here so long, there's no record of a time when they weren't here. Some forests in England were planted a few hundred years ago. Not this one. Some trees in here are so big that three people couldn't get their arms around them. Bigger, even."

"There're caves, even some old houses, like the woods sort of reached out and took them. It's gotten bigger than when I was a kid, I know that. Some farmers trim the edges, pull out new trees and stuff, keep their hedges straight, the trees fenced in. Not my Dad, though. He just lets it grow down here. We have other fields over the hill, he trims it back around them and by the house, but down here, we already lost a barn to the woods - see?"

He stopped his monologue and pointed over to the edge of the woods, a few hundred feet away from them. Charlotte could see a building inside the trees, kind of run down and collapsing.

"There's a lot of water underground and it's really swampy. Dad lets the woods grow here because we can't grow much in this field but grass and it's too hilly to get much hay. It's good, though. On the town side of the woods, the trees are dying. Too much pollution from the factory down there. You can't see it, but it spits out great clouds of stuff, and the trees don't like it. I see it as an exchange. We let the trees grow here because they're dying on the other side."

Mrs. Enright looked sideways at James. "Ever thought about being a conservationist, or a biologist or something? You should think about it, you seem to be so interested."

"No," said James, quite firmly. "I'm staying right here. Ted's off gallivanting around these days, he doesn't want to farm, but I don't mind. I'd rather just stay here. Maybe go to agricultural school or something. But I'm staying here, anyway." He dug his hands into his pockets and looked at the ground.

"Well," said Mrs. Enright, puzzled slightly by the outburst, "That's good, at least you know what you want. Unlike Charlotte, here."

Charlotte sighed and made a dour face.

They were reaching the edge of the trees, and Charlotte could see the dogs bounding through a gap in the hedge similar to her own.

"They know the way," laughed James.

"I want to go and see your caves," said Charlotte.

"Later," said James, "I promised to take your Mother to the river."

"Yes," said Mrs. Enright, "I want to see how far it is, maybe I can walk to town that way if it's shorter than the road."

"Much shorter," agreed James.

Charlotte wasn't having much fun. She stomped along behind everyone, looking around for things to come back to later. She started lagging further and further back, following along the path and listening to the drone of the conversation ahead. It was another pleasant day, with light fluffy clouds overhead. She could see the sky through the trees, this part of the woods was quite light and airy.

She'd been walking alone for about ten minutes, catching the occasional glimpse of James and her mother up ahead through the tree trunks. She was listening to the birds and the rustles in the bracken around her when she became aware that she could also hear other voices. Voices that were low and bubbly, like water, or like bees humming, rain falling, branches, musical voices all blurred in together.

58

She looked around but couldn't see anything at all out of the ordinary. She could hear James and her mother, closer now. They must have paused to let her catch up. She cocked her head to one shoulder, and listened intently. She could barely hear the buzzing of the other voices, but she was sure it was there. Perhaps there was a waterfall nearby, she thought. It sounded a lot like the humming she had heard before. She felt a tingling at the back of her neck and there was a surge in the strange noise. Just when she though she could actually pick out one voice from the background her Mother called "Charlotte... Charlotte... are you coming?" Everything else faded away.

The end of the town that was by the woods was quite different to the area around the school that Charlotte was used to seeing. Not many old houses here, not many new ones, either. Mainly it was big buildings with parking lots around them. The town had almost forty thousand people packed into it. The main business in the area was farming, and with the farming came the attendant industry. There was a dairy plant that processed milk, a meat packing plant, and a tannery. There were lots of warehouses and lorries bustled in and out of an industrial park. This end of town was further along the valley than the rest, and closer to the main road that went out to the coast. There were a few rows of grimy houses with cheerful window boxes and dry, pallid gardens.

James was pointing down stream. "You go around that bend there, the path's pretty good, and about half a mile farther there's the bridge to get into town."

The river was quite wide at this point. Charlotte realized that the streams by her house and the Starling's farm were only small feeder streams that emptied into the one big river that then flowed down to the sea. It was quite fast flowing, and about eight or nine yards across. She wondered how big it was in the other world, and then stopped herself. The other world was only a dream, she told herself.

"This is where I fish," said James. "Right here. Fishing's not too bad if you get here early enough in the morning or the right time in the evening. Downstream after it passes through more of the industrial area, the water's pretty filthy, and there's not many fish anymore."

They turned around and started back. Part of the way back, Charlotte's mother had an idea.

"Why don't we walk back through the woods, Charlotte, instead of going back to the farm and then home? Mrs. Starling and I said our goodbyes, let's just go home, we haven't had lunch yet and it's almost one."

"Um, sure, if you like."

"Well you can't get lost," laughed James. "Just come a bit farther with me and I'll show you a path that goes all the way through. It comes out by that gap in the hedge below your house."

"That's where I get in and out when I go for walks," said Charlotte.

"Some of these paths are old. These woods have been here so long that the animal paths have gotten wider and more packed down. Plus," he added "humans have been walking in these woods as long as the town's been here and some of the paths were manmade ages ago. Here's your one coming up now."

They walked around a bend and saw a track crossing the path they were on. It was quite well trodden and followed the edge of the trees inside the woods for about twenty-five feet or so. They said goodbye to James, and started along the path. Mrs. Enright was quietly planning a fast lunch and a couple of hours in the garden before supper.

The two of them walked silently through the woods, each lost in their own thoughts. Charlotte, of course, was trying to listen for the voices again and was grateful for her Mother's silence.

The path was easy, and went around the hill between the farm and the house instead of over it the way they had come. She made a note of it for future visits. She remembered seeing the other end of the path before. She had planned to follow it but she seemed always to end up wandering to the clearing, sitting under her favourite tree and daydreaming. She wondered about the missing dog, all those years ago.

Well, if James had been eleven, then it had been five years ago. Ken must only have been seven or eight. Poor Ken. 'I wonder why he never got another dog?' she thought. 'Should I tell him about the other Stig?'

And who was that old man in his house, anyway? He must be something to do with Ken's mysterious Great Grandfather, and perhaps with the Green man she kept seeing in the woods, too.

The path wound around a bend at the bottom of the hill, and the woods were full of blooms – one or two bluebells still stood, but there were other flowers dotted around the woods too, the trees were far apart here and let in a lot of light – even some grass grew.

"Charlotte?" asked her mother

"Hmm?"

"Do you want to help me pick an armful of these to take home?"

"Sure!" She brightened up a bit having something to do, and they spent ten minutes or so picking bundles of flowers. Charlotte hadn't been quite this far along her path before, she'd been at the other end. As they kept walking, the path became darker, the trees were thicker and let in less sunlight; there were fewer flowers and she walked further from the path to collect some of the ones that were still growing there.

The path hadn't rounded the hill yet, and it was colder further in. She could see the old ruined tree stump. It looked as if it didn't belong in these beautiful, peaceful woods. The more she looked at it, the more she started to see shadows moving around the stump, insubstantial shapes, perhaps just ferns moving in the breeze... but then, there was no breeze. Maybe animals. It seemed as though she was about to make something out of the shapes, then she shivered a little, involuntarily, and turned away to walk back to the path with her flowers.

As soon as she turned her back on the shadows, she became terrified of... Well, of something, anyway. Had she really seen anything around the old stump? If she had seen something, had it seen her?

61

She tried to run back to the path but found she was only capable of walking slowly, as if in a dream. She tried to walk faster but nothing happened. Her legs would not obey the panic stricken commands from her brain. It seemed like an age passed before she reached the path, and as soon as she did the feeling went away. She turned around. Nothing. The stump was just a slight irregularity in the trees, a darker spot amongst the shadows. Nothing moved. She walked over to where her mother was waiting.

They walked on. Charlotte was feeling better. She listened again for the voices, but heard nothing all the way back. Through the trees Charlotte could see the Starlings' cows. She tried to see if she could spot number 211. 'Too far to see,' she figured...

That night Charlotte again went to bed earlier than usual, much to the puzzlement of her parents. She fell asleep instantly, and almost right away began dreaming of the woods.

When she woke up, Charlotte was aware that it was not yet dawn. She wondered what had woken her, and remembered to look at her alarm clock. It was facing the right way this time, and it said five-o-clock.

'Five a.m.,' she thought, 'almost the same time as before'.

Her heart was pounding in her chest, and she could hear it loudly in her ears. It sounded like the rushing of feet through fallen leaves, someone walking towards her *sh-shhh, sh-shhh, sh-shhh*, louder and closer... 'It's just my heart beating,' she calmed herself. The rustling became fainter as she listened to the sounds in her room. The ticking of the clock was making her skin crawl with excitement.

'Someone's here,' she thought, remembering the feeling she had had before. 'Outside'. She got a strong image of the Green King in her head. 'If I look out the window he'll be there'. She was exhilarated by the thought of finding out the truth, of seeing the Green King in front of her eyes, not from the corners, or in dreams, but really truly there.

Charlotte hesitated a moment, but the temptation was too great. She sat up, and put her feet on the floor and heard a

62

sound, this time it was the same sound she'd heard in the woods. Low, gurgling voices.

She pinched herself to see if she was awake, and the pain reassured her that everything was real. The noise became louder, and the room began to fill up with the same smell that was in the clearing and Ken's ruins.

Her bedroom window had been left open as the weather was so warm, and a slow breeze was moving her curtains. Outside she could hear the chestnut tree moving against the window.

'Funny,' she thought, 'the branch that touches the window is tiny, this sounds so much larger.'

She got up and put on her clothes, then went to the window. By now, the breeze was almost a wind, and the curtains were blowing away from the window. Dawn was coming earlier and earlier this time of year, and the sky was quite bright. In the brackish grey light she could see that the tree was moving, writhing around freely. She sensed great waves of joy and contentment coming from the tree, like a language of emotion. She stepped closer to the window.

The Green King was standing under the tree outside her window. He was closer than he had ever been. He was looking up at her window smiling and waving.

"Come down," he said, inside her head. "There are things you must see, the morning is beautiful."

The tree sent a happy shout to her - "Come down!" it radiated. "Beautiful," it echoed.

Charlotte felt light and buoyant, as if she could float right out of the window down to the earth like a feather. She smiled and leaned out of the window.

"Don't jump, foolish one!" said the Green King. "Let the tree help you."

The girl leaned further out and giggled, "I'm not jumping, I'm just looking." The sound of her voice surprised her, it was the loudest sound in the morning silence.

"Speak with your mind, I can understand you," he said.

"Like this?" she thought.

"Yes."

63

Charlotte felt a bubbling volcano of happiness well up from her stomach. She felt so good. The air was warm and inviting, the light was mysterious and promising. She looked at the wood and saw that it was surrounded by the wall she had seen the day she met the old man with the dog up at Ken's house. He was beckoning to her. The tree reached out its branch, which was thick and strong. She swung her legs over her windowsill, unafraid. The branch wove through the air until it was underneath her. She tiptoed onto it carefully, and crouched down until she was sitting on it. It started to move gently towards the ground.

The tree was sending out blasts of happy, uncomplicated thoughts all about how wonderful the sunshine was, how glad it was she could ride on it, how fresh the air was. As the branch reached the ground, Charlotte practically danced off it, full of all the happiness of life. The branch swung gently back into place and shrank back to its regular size. I must be dreaming thought Charlotte again.

"You're not dreaming, little one, you're just looking at the world with your other eyes. Or perhaps you'd like to think of it as looking into another world. Your world and my world are very similar. They are almost the same in many ways, but they are drifting farther and farther apart."

Charlotte settled down in the grass at the foot of the tree. She listened, and the Green King told her a story.

"Once, there was only one world, here on Earth. Many people but one world. Not so long ago, either. Gradually a change began to occur. Human beings have become more and more violent, more and more concerned with building and owning and fighting than over living peacefully with the land and each other. People have always fought battles, it's not a new thing. Ever since the beginning of the human race, the world has begun to split. For the animals and the plants, for everything except man, there is still only one world, but for man, there are now three."

"Man is the only animal capable of evil for its own sake, and man is the only animal that knows the concept of money. Money is the reason that most evil is committed.

64

Money is the reason for most pollution, most crime, most of the reasons that the dark world exists. Without man, there would be no need for my world or the dark world, there would only be one world. There are some very rare people who can't tell the difference between my world and yours, or our worlds and the dark world, but most of them are considered insane and locked away. More and more power is being given to the dark world by mankind, and the more powerful the dark world becomes, the higher the chances of it flowing over into your world, and eventually into mine."

"But," said Charlotte, her voice sounding very loud, "your world is so beautiful. Do all the good things make your world stronger? Why did the good things split... oh. I see. You left because of all the bad things..."

"That's right," said the Green King, speaking inside her head. "Both the light and the dark worlds were born at the same time. For ages the balance has been kept, but recently things have become worse and the dark world threatens to take over."

Charlotte was a little puzzled. She spoke with her mind again even though they had walked away from the house and couldn't be heard. "You mean... I mean... If there are three worlds, how come you never hear about it... are the other worlds inside the earth? Is this something like science fiction, another dimension? Or is it like, the afterlife, heaven, you know..."

"It's as if you had three pieces of tissue paper, each of which had the Earth drawn on them. When you put them together and shine a light through them, it looks just like one picture. Then, on one drawing you add houses and cities and things, and you don't draw anything on the others. When you shine the light through them, you see the one image with cities on it, but underneath you know there are other, cleaner maps."

"Are there some things on all the maps? What's on the dark world? How do you get from your world to mine? Is your world just hills and rivers and stuff, nature?"

"No. Some buildings exist in all the worlds, although not

very many. In this part of the world, the ruins in the woods that you saw the other day are a doorway. We have a few buildings all over the world, some built in your world, some built in ours from your stone. Some exist as gates between your world and ours, and some, like the ruins, exist in all three worlds. These are rare, and very useful. They act as windows on all the worlds, but can only be used by people with... certain abilities." The Green King stopped.

"So, if I build a house in my world out of stone from yours, would it be a doorway too?"

"Sort of." He smiled. "You figure things out pretty quickly, don't you?"

Charlotte went on. "What about wood? If I took a branch from the woods on my side into your side, would it act as a door too, instead of a stone building?" she asked.

"Close, a key. But it would work best with something that originates in your world and doesn't exist in the others. When you're in one world, anything from the other acts as a door, or the key to the door. It is easier and safer if you have an actual building and know how to use it, or, with a lot of concentration you can work with anything, but it's harder and very dangerous. Many of those who cross over become lost, sometimes unable to ever cross back."

"Is that why children have gone missing?" asked Charlotte, nervously.

"Sometimes, yes. We rescue any that we can."

Charlotte shivered at the thought of what that might mean, what might have happened to those who couldn't be rescued... where they might have gone. The Green King continued.

"I know what people are saying. We do not take any that do not beg to come and even then we only take those who, like yourself, are one of us. Some people have crossed to our world and stayed, but we never take children." The Green King was stern and clearly very angry about the things people had been saying. Charlotte was embarrassed that she had asked.

Charlotte wanted to know how she could be one of them

when clearly she was human, had been born in London and had never even seen the woods until recently. Instead, she kept quiet and asked a simpler question, one which she was dying to know. "What do you use as a key to get back and forth?" she asked. The Green King chuckled to himself.

"I don't need to use anything," he said, laughing, "I can use myself, for I am a key!"

"What do you mean?" she wanted to know, but he wouldn't answer.

The sun was higher on the horizon, beginning to poke itself right out into the open. "I," said the Green King finally, "am King over all the woods. My Lady wife is Queen, the summer is her season, the winter, mine; we exist everywhere but you can find us in the clearing. She has found the trees dying this year, more than ever before and has asked me to help her. The woods are getting weak."

A great wave of sadness overtook Charlotte suddenly, she felt heavy, lost, weak. She looked at the Green King, and he saw she was upset.

"Don't feel pity for us, my friend, we aren't dying as fast as you are. When your people have died out, we will still be here - but alone and in a world not as beautiful as it is even now, a world desolate and barren. People, humans, have to be aware. We need more on our side, you people need to learn the danger we are all in... So by helping us, you help yourselves." There was a long pause while Charlotte thought over all the things she had just been told. Clearly the woods were in danger, and so, in some way, was her own world.

Suddenly the Green King began laughing again; he seemed unable to be serious for long. "Well, hurry up, I'm off," he said, and disappeared right in front of her eyes.

The breeze that had died down while she talked to the Green King began to rise up again, and the tree began to quiet its movements. As it had become larger when the Green King arrived, so it now became smaller, until it looked exactly the same as it did every day. The air began to smell more like it usually did - of wet grass and cow sheds - and the sun got brighter and brighter.

The birds were singing the dawn chorus, and as they did every morning they woke up Roger, and the dog woofed to be let outside. She walked back to the house, went inside and left a note for her parents, then took Roger on a pre-breakfast ramble.

Chapter 6

The day was shaping up to be another scorcher and a good morning for a stroll to the clearing. Charlotte and the dog made their way there, and she sat down under her favourite tree - her favourite mainly because it had a comfortable root to lean against, a big one with just the right curve in it for her back.

It was also close enough to the stream running in the clearing that if she bought a cup, she could lean over and scoop some of the beautifully sweet, cold, clean water whenever she was thirsty. The air smelt so good, it made her feel alive, alert. She leaned back against the root, crossed her arms behind her head, and waited to see what would happen.

'I wonder where the Green King is?' thought Charlotte. 'He said I'd find them in the clearing.' She was pretty sure that 'us' meant him and the other green people and then she realised what he had said. 'Hurry Up'. 'Find us'. He wanted her to try to find them on her own – but without a key… No, she knew what to do. She sat back and thought very hard, trying to see the trees waving in the other world, trying to listen for the voice of the Green King. She began to hear a low murmur over the trickling of the stream, the now familiar sound of voices.

A voice in her ear shouted 'Boo!' She jumped, looked behind her, nothing. It too had been a girl's voice, familiar, somehow.

"Who's there?" asked Charlotte in a small voice. "Who are you?"

She heard laughter again, this time laughter from lots of voices.

And then there were people.

Green people, flesh and blood, looking at her quietly, smiling. A girl walked out from behind her: Gaua from her dream. The Green King was there, too, but his old clothes were gone, replaced with a long cape made from the same soft green and brown hued cloth as before, tailored into a magnificent outfit, trimmed with all sorts of different feathers. Charlotte was so busy taking it all in that she almost missed the moment when a woman appeared standing beside the Green King. A tall woman, beautiful, in a gown of the same fabric. She glowed with her own light, and seemed to look right inside Charlotte's head.

"Welcome," said the lady. "Welcome home."

It echoed around the clearing "Welcome home... Welcome home", many different voices this time.

"You are one of us. You have always been one of us. We've been waiting."

Charlotte was staring slack-jawed at the vision in front of her. The woman seemed to be so large, and yet still so delicate and willowy. She was paler than most of the others, but rather than being green, she appeared to be all colours, as if the surface of her skin were constantly shifting hues.

She shook herself out of her stupor and stood up, self-consciously brushing leaves from her jeans, and looking around for Roger. His tail was brushing uncertainly back and forth across the primroses, and he was looking at the couple in front of them. Actually, he was looking at the dog that was standing between them. Charlotte noticed the animal finally. It was staring intently at Roger, but the Green King had his hand on the animal's head, stopping it from running over to touch noses. Charlotte then noticed the man she had met at Ken's 'other' house was standing behind the couple. He smiled at her.

Charlotte could see everything so clearly. The smell of the air was overpoweringly beautiful. It smelt sweet, clean, the same as the clearing always smelt but... more so. She didn't know what to do. Everyone was just looking at her, waiting for her to say something. They were all relaxed and smiling, as if they'd been expecting her.

The tall woman in front of her reached out a hand.

"Come on, we won't bite, you know," she laughed gently. Charlotte had a strong feeling that the woman was extremely important. More important than a king or queen, more important than anyone famous, the most important person she'd ever meet ever. She tried to smile but she found herself too surprised and nervous and scared to move.

As she became more afraid, she could feel something moving around outside the circle of trees. She tried to concentrate on the green people but it became harder and harder. She was becoming more and more frightened. With the fear came uncertainty. Was she just dreaming? Had she fallen asleep? Grey tendrils began to waft through the trees. The people started fading away, and what ever was outside the clearing was becoming stronger, reaching through the trees and draining away her energy. It became harder and harder to see the Green King and his lady. She felt faint, as though she was going to pass out.

'No,' she thought, 'Not again'. She drew in a slow deep breath and shut her eyes. She concentrated upon staying alert, making the dizziness go away.

Dimly, from around the clearing came the voices of the Green people.

"She's fading... Charlotte... Charlotte... Concentrate... Come on girl..." They ebbed and flowed, first getting stronger and louder, and then fading into a whisper, fading away almost to nothing and then coming in again, like she was picking up a weak radio signal on her stereo.

A radio signal.

As Charlotte concentrated on not giving in to the tentacles of fear that reached through from beyond the trees she realized that the voices were actually quite like a radio signal, but that the receiver the was her mind. She figured out that when she concentrated on the smell of the air in the clearing, and on the buzzing of the green people's voices, they became clearer, louder, more distinct. When she thought about the thing outside the trees, whatever it was became stronger and her vision would start to fade. The sun would dim, and begin to disappear behind the trees, which would become thicker, taller. The soft green underbrush would fade and be replaced by clouds of something thick and thorny looking.

She realised she was seeing another, darker, wood. It was

colder and somehow menacing and she started to shake. She concentrated on the bright, safe, warm wood and the green people. She realized that tuning her mind to the safe signal made the dangerous one fade away. She wrenched her thoughts away from the dark woods and started thinking in detail about the green people, the woman she had seen, the Green King himself, and soon she began to see them again.

Things became solid and substantial again and she was back in the summer day, in the clearing, with Roger, and the Green King.

Everyone else had moved out of the clearing, they were on their own.

"Very good Charlotte. I'm sorry we made you do this on your own but I wanted you to realise that you must be very careful," announced the Green King in a strong, low voice. The sound startled Charlotte, she had never heard the sound of him speaking before, except in her head. He noticed the look on her face and smiled.

"There are things you must learn. It isn't safe while you are crossing between the woods. In your woods, or in mine, you are perfectly alright. In the journey between the two there are dangers. That was the other world. It can't reach into our world here at all, just as we cannot cross over into that world. Both sides can get into your world but the dark world cannot come here and we cannot go there.

"Between the woods however it is a different story. Anyone travelling between the worlds could be pulled into either one. Just as someone falling into that dark world can get pulled in to our world, so someone trying to get to my woods," he motioned to the woods in which they were standing – "can be grabbed by that side if they are not concentrating hard enough."

At this, Charlotte felt a flush of fear rise up from the soles of her feet. The Green King was staring quite hard at her. She knew exactly what he was trying to say. He was trying to say that if she was grabbed by the dark when she was crossing over, she might get dragged in, and the Green King couldn't go into the other side to help her.

Those tentacles of fear were real, or as real as she believed the Green King's woods to be; and with him standing before her in the flesh she could hardly doubt the existence of his woods. Therefore what he was saying was very likely true, and she was extremely frightened. She looked down at the grass between her feet, looked over at Roger who was sitting a few feet away studying her intently, and looked back at the Green King.

"Can I get back, if... um..."

"If the other side takes you," interrupted the Green King, "you are not powerless, but you have to listen to me." He sat down on the exposed roots of the tree next to Charlotte's. Roger padded over and lay down between them, looking intently at the other dog, Stig. The Green King noticed her glance and said softly, "It is different for animals. They have not drawn any lines, their minds are freer, they have no problem being in both worlds at once."

"Are there animals in the... um... other world, the darker one, too?" asked Charlotte.

"Not really. Most animals don't understand good and evil enough to choose between the two. They know they would rather be warm than cold, fed than hungry, comfortable than uncomfortable. They can sense the other world and it frightens them. Some predatory animals don't seem to be as bothered by it but most won't stay there. Oh, a few insects and birds and some small mammals survive quite happily there, they're not evil as such, but that world is just... suited to them."

Charlotte shivered, imagining things that feed on dead things, rotten wood... dead... she didn't really want to think about it.

"Fear is one of the things that is very strong in that wood," he continued. "Sometimes there is nothing to be afraid of in there, but fear itself is walking around. It's not necessarily unsafe on that side, it's just frightening. If you were there, you would be filled with fear and would be too frightened to be able to concentrate on getting home. If you are ever caught on the other side you would have to concentrate on

73

this world, your own world. Hold on to a key, you can even use your clothing if you have to, anything that was made in your world will work. Just hold it, concentrate on it and how it belongs to your world. Think about your parents, your friends, all things that belong to your world, and your own world will get stronger for you."

"Remember you cannot get from that world straight to mine, only to your own. And just as I am able to walk freely in your world if I want, so can the other side, but it is hard for them. It is hard for most of us, also."

"There used to be no intelligence on the other side at all, just a senseless, formless evil, like a mass of poisonous jelly, or a cloud. Its nature was to grow, to destroy, like setting fire to a piece of paper - the fire will burn the paper, not because it hates the paper but because it's stronger and can't help it. Sometimes it seeps out into your world and terrible things happen – wars, pestilence, it escapes all the time."

"Now, we sense that for the first time, actual creatures from the dark side are trying to escape into your world. Anything managing to live in that side must be pretty nasty. There wasn't anything there at all until a few hundred years ago and we don't know what they are. We need human help to find out. We have to find some way to get them, or it, into your world where we can destroy it. Some one has to go in after it."

Charlotte didn't like the way the conversation was going, but when she looked around, the day was still bright and the clearing was still beautiful.

"The other side is just like fire to your paper. We are water, the flip side, the opposite. Right now, we are safe from the other side, it is safe from us. Your world is the battle ground. We need your help. If the other world ever takes over your world it is then possible for it to reach into ours."

Charlotte felt chilled. She was pretty dumbfounded by all the information. She thought for a minute in silence, the Green King looking on. "If they can reach into my world, then why don't they? Why haven't I ever seen any of them, or felt anything?"

74

"But you have," retorted the Green King. "Every time you saw me, or thought you heard voices you became dizzy. The first time you saw me through your window you were very frightened but you didn't know why. That was the other side leaking through the hole you made around yourself, making you afraid. You would pass out. Passing out is a common reaction to fear."

"Unless you are already on the other side when you faint, you will naturally wake up in your own world, but if you are too far over into the other side, you will be caught. If you are, it's best to take a few deep breaths and concentrate on your house – remember, use a key – it could be anything. Your trainers, your mobile phone, something that is from your own world. If you are caught by the other side and it takes everything from you it will be very hard, almost impossible for you to cross back."

"But I was born in my world, am I not a key to it just like you are to yours?"

"No child, we are different. You are human and like any animal your body can exist in any world at all, it's just your mind which is attuned to your own world and if you had nothing with you at all, it is only your mind that can bring you back. Here are some things you need to know."

"If you are in the woods, try to get out. They are the same shape as the ones in your world but just a bit bigger. Find a path you know is a way out and stick to it, don't step off it, and walk, don't run. When you run you raise the level of adrenalin in your body. Adrenalin is something your brain sends to your body to make it energetic. It's also something your brain releases when you are afraid."

"If you raise the adrenalin in your body by running you will become more afraid and you will pass out. If you pass out on the other side it will try to immobilize you with fear and keep you that way for a long time. You will need great strength to overcome the fear. Without a key it will be extremely difficult. Outside of the woods you will be safer."

"How can I stop it from happening every time I cross into your woods?" asked Charlotte.

"I am going to give you a gift. With it you will be able to cross the barriers between your world and mine with greater ease, and it will also act as a guard against the other world."

The Green King reached into his cloak. Charlotte hadn't seen any pockets there but there must have been a large one, as he pulled out a big, square piece of cloth and handed it to her. It felt like the softest silk, and was as light as air. It was quite large, large enough for Charlotte to wrap around her body like a big bath towel, but so fine it could be wound into a thin rope.

"Tie this around you. With it you will be able to concentrate on our world, and the other will not be able to reach through it to get you. Think of it as a shield and don't lose it whatever you do."

The Green King eyed her steadily for a moment, as if to impress upon her the importance of what he was saying. He lifted up his head and sniffed the air and then he looked at her and grinned. "I," he announced, "am off. Coming?" With that he rippled a little, as if she was seeing at his reflection in water, and suddenly she was looking right into the eyes of the old grey stag. It regarded her for a second, tossed its head and she swore that she saw one of its eyes close in a wink. It knelt down in front of her and the Green King's voice rang in her head.

"Get on," it ordered.

Uncertain of what she had heard, Charlotte hesitated for a second.

"Get on," it repeated. "On my back!"

Charlotte took a faltering step towards the animal. Close up it smelt vaguely of leaves and straw, capped off with a strong, musky animal smell. She walked up until she was standing beside the deer. Even through it was kneeling in a most un-deer-like manner, it still stood higher than her waist. She knotted the cloth around her neck and moved closer, still uncertain.

"Don't be afraid, I am plenty strong enough to hold you," laughed the voice of the Green King. "Grab my neck, come on girl, this may be your one and only chance to ride a deer!

76

I won't let you fall."

Charlotte swallowed once, steadied her nerves, and by clasping her arms around the animal's neck, she hauled herself up onto its back. Below her Roger was woofing softly and wagging his tail, nose to nose with the shadow of a dog, the wispiest outline of the other animal visible.

"Hold on... here we go!" laughed the voice as the old deer started to move.

It was the most graceful ride Charlotte could ever remember having. She had taken riding lessons on holiday and was pretty steady on horseback, but she had never ridden without a saddle and she was nervous about her ability to stay on.

All her fears were unnecessary. The ride was quite unlike a horse. The deer picked up its feet very carefully, its back barely moved. It was so big that she could have lain down and slept. She leaned forward and wrapped her arms more firmly around his neck.

They left the clearing and began picking their way delicately through the underbrush and over to the path. As the animal picked up the pace she felt jubilant. Here she was, riding through the woods aback a deer. Unheard of. She could see Roger running along, and as she watched, the other dog came into view. They were running behind, letting out the occasional bark, wandering into the underbrush and crashing back, tails dragging tendrils of ferns and brambles. She wondered briefly why Roger was so uninterested in the deer. Usually if dogs smelt deer they would go flying off after them, hot on the scent, but these two seemed well aware of the true nature of this particular deer and were far more interested in chasing each other and peeing on trees.

The end of the path drew near and Charlotte could see the edge of the wood. They were bounding now, faster and faster towards the gate. As they got there, it opened and they bounded out into the field. Charlotte was amazed at how easy it was. She knew that riding any other deer would be different - in fact, even if one could get close enough to ride a deer, no deer would be patient enough to carry a human -

and she knew that the Green King was balancing her very carefully. It was exhilarating.

The Green King slowed. Charlotte was laughing and hot, the dogs were careening around, chasing each other, rolling over in a heap and wagging furious tails, dashing off in another direction - totally ignoring the girl and the deer. They were going slower and slower now, the deer giving off a moist heat, tossing his head and blowing through his nose. He stopped, knelt down again, and Charlotte dismounted. Her own world began to appear again, her house, the garden, everything. The grass looked positively grey in comparison. Then it was just Charlotte and the deer and Roger, still racing circles around the field.

The deer looked once over its shoulder and headed off into the woods. Charlotte didn't see Ken, looking over the Enrights' garden wall in astonishment, looking at the deer - by now almost back in the trees - looking at Charlotte and most of all, looking at Roger, past Roger at something else, at another dog that was now running behind the deer, nearly invisible to everyone except Roger and the Green King. And Ken.

It was Sunday morning. So much had happened to Charlotte already that weekend that she couldn't get excited about school being almost over. One more week. The summer loomed ahead of her, full of promises and amazement.

She trudged the rest of the way up the hill to the garden wall. She realized that she had no idea of the time, that she might have even missed breakfast. She reached the gate and climbed over. She could see her mother's back, bent over a seedbed, digging and planting in the vegetable garden beside the house. As she walked up to the house her father came out of the kitchen door and walked around the tree to meet her.

"So you're back hmmm? Took your time... we just sent Ken looking for you."

"Was he here?" asked Charlotte

"Still is, I think... He went down through the gate, I'm

surprised you didn't meet him on the way." Her father knitted his brow slightly, perplexed.

"Should I go after him?" she asked, hoping she was going to be able to stay home and eat.

"Well, I should think so, he's gone looking for you, after all."

"But I haven't eaten yet, I'm starved..." Charlotte almost mentioned that she had felt dizzy again in the woods, but stopped herself in time as she remembered both the real reason for the dizzy spell and then that she would be kept inside again if her parents thought she was sick.

"Look, if you run after him now you'll catch him in no time. Really, he just left, he probably isn't even in the woods yet. Run!"

With that order, she ran down to the bottom of the garden and hopped back over the gate. She didn't have to go very far in order to find Ken. He was sitting by the wall partially hidden behind an elderberry bush. His arms were wrapped around his legs and he was leaning his head on his knees. He had a very peculiar look on his face. Embarrassed slightly, she cleared her throat and asked if she could sit with him.

"Alright," he said in a low voice.

Charlotte sat beside him for a moment, leaned back against the wall and didn't say anything. She too was thinking. If Ken had been sent down to the gate to get her, then he must have seen her appear in the field, may even have seen the deer. She wondered how she could find out what he had seen without giving anything away.

"Anything wrong?" she asked, trying to make her voice sound as non-committal as possible. She faced forward, not looking at Ken, not wanting to make him uncomfortable.

Ken stirred beside her, she sensed he was looking at her and she turned her head. He stared at her seriously for quite a while, then looked away, staring back over the fields. Across the small valley she could see the Starlings' cows grazing on the slope below the sheds. She watched for a while, half hoping to be able to spot people, searching through the cows for number 211. Beside her, Ken cleared his throat.

"I saw you with the deer."

Charlotte jumped slightly. Could Ken see into that other wood? Could he have seen her riding the stag?

"Well," she said a little angrily, "what did you see, then?"

Ken looked at her again, this time he was almost smiling.

"Don't get your knickers in a twist then, I won't tell anyone."

"Tell anyone what?" she asked, trying to keep her voice from trembling.

"Nothing. Just that I saw you in the field with that old grey stag..." his voice trailed off, he stopped for a moment. "Um, remember that dog I had that went missing?"

That was it. The dog hadn't gone missing, it had somehow crossed over to the other woods and stayed there. Charlotte had known it was Ken's dog. After she had gotten off the deer and back into the real world, she couldn't see the animal at all. How, then, did Ken see it? Ken must have been able to see into the bright world, even through he probably didn't realise it. She smiled.

"Was that your dog that was with Roger?" she asked brightly. Ken was looking at her strangely, slightly puzzled.

"Well, it looked like him, but that was four years ago. He was old when he disappeared... I had him from a puppy when I was a baby, we grew up together." The boy was silent for a second.

"He'd be same age as me, almost fourteen. Old for a dog. That dog was young, looked like a puppy. Same colour though... and Stig had one white ear, same as that dog..."

"Well," said Charlotte, "Maybe Stig did just run away, or got lost or something. Maybe he met another wild dog and they had puppies or something. This could be his puppy…"

"Yeah maybe," grunted Ken.

"Or, I don't know. That dog's called Stig, too, you know," said Charlotte, softly.

"Really? How do you know?" asked Ken.

Charlotte thought for a moment, debating whether or not to tell Ken what she knew.

Just then Charlotte's stomach, which had been grumbling

gently, let out a really loud moaning sound. She laughed, embarrassed.

"Haven't had breakfast yet, have you?" said Ken. "Bet you don't even know what time it is, either?" he added.

"No," admitted Charlotte. "What time is it, anyway?"

"Eleven o'clock."

"What?!" She leapt to her feet. She'd left the house at eight, and although a lot had happened it had all seemed to happen very fast, she had thought it was maybe nine-thirty, ten o'clock.

"Almost, anyway," said Ken, checking his wrist. "Your Mum invited me back for lunch if I wanted. I haven't eaten yet either..." He glanced sideways at Charlotte. She smiled at him and reached down to help him up.

"Come on then, let's see if we can eat outside and talk."

The two of them went inside. Mr. Enright followed them in and fixed them a late breakfast of eggs, toast and fried potatoes.

"Your Mother and I are going across to the Starlings' again today to pick up those hens; soon we'll have eggs of our own," Mr. Enright told Charlotte as he was cooking. "I finished the chicken shed yesterday, did you see it?"

"No," said Charlotte, "where did you put it?"

"You!" said her dad, laughing. "You don't pay attention to anything, do you! It's in the corner of the garden closest to the house. You just walked right past it. I'm going to reinforce the gate with chicken wire so they can't get into the field, and then they'll have the run of the place."

"You're going to let them run anywhere they want?" asked Charlotte, amazed.

"Haven't you ever heard of free-range hens?" asked Ken with a bit of a sneer.

"No," she answered, darting a dagger glance his way.

"Come on, you two. Go outside and eat this," said Mr. Enright, handing them each a plate, cutlery and napkins. They went outside and sat down on the lawn chairs in the shade of the chestnut tree. The weather was lovely.

"If it stays like this all summer, I'm going to get a tan,"

said Charlotte, happily.

"You're not getting anything if you spend all your time in them woods, you know," interjected Ken. She laughed, self-consciously.

"Well, I like to stay in the clearing. There's plenty of sun gets through there. Besides, YOU spend all your time in there and YOU have a tan..."

Ken looked at her steadily for a moment as he munched on some toast. He put down his plate and rolled up the sleeve of his T-shirt. "I'm this colour all over," he said. "It's not a tan."

"Wow. Your mother and sister are so pale..." Charlotte said, suddenly worried she was saying something wrong, that maybe Ken was adopted and didn't want to talk about it.

"So's me Dad. I look like my great-grandfather. He was really dark. Me Grandmother was darker too, apparently. She was born in my house. It's really old. Bet I'm the only person you know whose family has lived in one house for a hundred years."

"Wow!" Charlotte was impressed. "Mind you, this used to be my great great great Gran's house or something." Ken raised an eyebrow as she continued, "Do you really not know where your great-granddad came from originally?"

"No one knows. There's some old papers in the library. There was some sort of scandal when he bought the house. He... well... he just moved in, and then went looking for the owner. It was empty for a few years. He restored it, added to it a bit, knocked a few bits down and I don't think he ever paid for it, really. He gave the town some money, I think. It used to be the house belonging to someone who didn't like the Porters very much a long, long time ago. The whole family disappeared one day. Everyone thought the Porters had done it, but that was that. Then my Granddad moved in and we've been there ever since."

"But, you mean no-one knows where he came from, your grand... great granddad?"

"Nope. But he had a lot of money and he married the Porters' daughter."

"Really? Your Great Grandmother was a Porter? So you should have inherited the woods, and the house, and, everything..." Charlotte was stunned.

"Naw. She was the last one, the only child they had. The old man was pretty rotten, cut her off for marrying... marrying my Grandad, I suppose." Ken chuckled and polished off another forkful of eggs. He didn't seem to care a whit about the loss of all that money. It was an awfully long time ago, Charlotte supposed. "When he died he left everything to the town except that he let his wife live in the big house until she died before the town could get it. It's full of stuff from their house. We have a few things but most of the valuable stuff is in the museum. They built this town, you know."

"I guessed that," Charlotte replied, thinking of all the local place names that referred to the Porter family.

"They wanted to rename the town *Porterfield* but it had been around for a few hundred years before that and no one would let them. Mad about that, they were. They just made it bigger, prosperous. In the cloth trade, they were."

"How come you know so much?" asked Charlotte.

Ken was wiping the last piece of his toast around the plate. He put it in his mouth and munched for a while. Charlotte followed suit. She had slowed down her eating while Ken talked so as not to appear too greedy, and the last piece of potato had been sitting forlornly on her plate for a while. Ken finished chewing and had a drink of water and said, "Me Mum knows the stories, plus I've been to the museum a lot, sort of me family home and all that. I read all the old papers a year or two ago. Wanted to know everything. I was trying to find out who my Great-granddad really was, if you want to know. He appeared from no-where, almost. Maybe Spanish, or something. Mum says people thought he was a pirate. Maybe we can go to the museum sometime?"

"Sure," she said.

"Maybe," Ken continued, "maybe at the same time you can tell me what you know about the woods. Maybe you can tell me what you were doing riding that deer AND how you

83

know the name of that dog."

In the silence that followed Charlotte noticed Ken looking at the scarf still knotted around her neck, and belatedly noticed the fabric of the T-shirt he was wearing, the t-shirt he always wore. It was so faded that it looked white, so faded that the original colour was difficult to see, so thin and fine that you couldn't really even tell how green it had been originally.

Chapter 7

That week at school went by really slowly. Charlotte spent quite a bit of time with Rosemary and Ken, the first quite amused by the second, the second a little perplexed by the first.

"Told you he was after you!" giggled Rosemary in the corner of the playing field one lunch hour as they watched Ken sitting against the wall of the school staring off into space.

Charlotte had just imparted the news that Ken had asked her to go to the museum with him, and Rosemary was both amused and impressed. Ken was a little strange but intelligent and good looking and it hadn't gone unnoticed by the other girls in the school.

Charlotte didn't like any of the boys at all. Instead, she and Rosemary spent much of their time talking about Tony and Ken, with Rosemary making elaborate plans to follow Tony around without being too obvious. Both boys hung out with large groups playing football or running around.

Tony still played marbles sometimes with the younger boys and Rosemary and Charlotte would join the groups of onlookers for a few minutes. After a while, Tony had given Rosemary a couple for her own and crouched behind her offering instructions on how to aim and fire successfully. After that, Rosemary could no longer be counted on to talk to Charlotte until school was over, and Charlotte would either sit beside the school and study or go and talk with some of the other girls.

Because it was the last week of school, everyone was in high spirits. Plans were being made for the summertime, telephone numbers were being exchanged. Charlotte got invitations to a few birthday parties over the holidays and promised to have people over to her house one day. In the summer the town opened up an outdoor pool and everyone would spend the summer in the sun, swimming and eating ice cream. There was going to be lots to do.

The final couple of days in school were almost over.

Charlotte handed in her last assignments. There were school games and no real work was being done. Charlotte entered the hurdling competition for her house because she was very fast, and her team won. Rosemary and Ken were both in a different house. Rosemary came in third in her swimming race and Ken came in first in a 100-metre run. On Thursday, shortly after she had run her race Charlotte ran into James on the playing field.

"Hi!" she said brightly.

"Hello Charlotte, I hear you won, congratulations!"

"Thanks."

"I'm glad to run into you," he said, "I was going to ask you if you still wanted to go exploring. I'm busy most of Saturday, but Sunday I thought maybe we could take the dogs."

"You mentioned caves, once. Are there really caves in there?"

James was silent for a moment. A worried look crossed his face. "Well, they're not really safe... but I know them quite well. I'll take you there, if you like. Remember to bring a torch."

"OK, " she said, feeling a little excited.

At the end of the day, Rosemary and Ken's house - the Red house - had come first, and Charlotte's had come second. Rosemary sought her out after the bell rang. "Well, we won but I didn't help much!" she laughed self-consciously.

"Rubbish. The water was freezing. Besides, it's only a stupid game, anyway."

Rosemary looked away, embarrassed. "You can talk. Tony was watching you run, he said you're the fastest. You and Ken!"

"Get out of here!" giggled Charlotte. "Speaking about fast, you and Tony sure disappeared quickly at lunch!"

Rosemary blushed happily. "He wants me to go out with him all summer!" The girls laughed and walked to the bus stop. "No ride home today?" asked Charlotte.

"Naw, Simon's got a date with the girl from the sweet shop." Rosemary laughed out loud. "Tony says he's at his house getting ready just like a girl! He's not picking her up 'til six but he said he didn't have time to drive us all around. Tomorrow night he's going to take me and Tony to a movie!"

Charlotte was happy for her friend. Her parents probably wouldn't let her do anything like that, she thought, and then she remembered that they were letting her go to the museum with Ken sometime, and that was almost as good. She waved goodbye to Rosemary when the bus came, and sat and thought about things on the way home.

She decided that she wanted to find out more about the other areas in the woods, like the ruined house that Ken liked so much, and James' caves.

She piled down the stairs in an old pair of jeans and ran into the living room where her mother was reading. "Can I go into the woods?"

"Alright, just be back in time to help me with the chickens. They're supposed to be your chore you know," she yelled after Charlotte's rapidly retreating back.

Charlotte ran upstairs and climbed out of her school clothes, called for the dog and started down the garden to the gate. Most of the clouds had cleared away without raining at all and the late afternoon sun was warm. There was no breeze blowing at all, everything was very still.

Halfway to the gate she remembered the scarf and ran back inside to get it. She had hung it carefully in her closet under a winter coat and it was still there. As she knotted it around her neck, out of sight under her t-shirt, she remembered Ken's shirt. She looked out of the side window over to the top side of the woods, where Ken spent his time. She decided she was going to try and find the old ruined house and see what she could find.

Roger was surprised when she went into the upper field beside the house and not down to the usual gap. He kept running down the slope and she had to call him back. He finally wheeled around and went barrelling off ahead of her sniffing along the edges of the hedgerows quite happily.

Charlotte thought about Ken.

Could Ken cross over into the other side at will? Where did he get his shirt? How much did he know about the Green people? It was quite a way to the top gap in the hedge, and as she trudged across the field, her mind went in circles. She remembered the dark cloud that had come out of this same gap a few days ago, and was a little hesitant to go boldly walking in. She paused for a moment, but she knew she'd be safe in the trees. Her scarf sat comfortably on her neck.

She looked at her watch. Quarter to five. Dinner was at six thirty and she had to be back by six to help her mother feed the hens. She wished she hadn't been so enthusiastic about offering to help before. Making the mash was a nasty, messy job – cooking up leftover people food and smashing it into mush.

It seemed so long ago that she had arrived in this town and she had changed so much. When she first moved she had emailed all her friends every night, chatted online, texted them secretly in class but recently she had been in touch less and less often. How could she explain all this to her friends in London? 'Oh sure,' she thought. 'Dear Beth. The woods here are full of trees that move all by themselves. I met an old Green King who turned into a deer and I rode on his back. I'm learning how to cross into this other world and I've seen what fear looks like.' They'd think she was crazy. 'Maybe I am...' she thought to herself.

It was five to five when she reached the gap. The path beyond it looked quite like the one she used, and knew she could find the house.

The path wound under the trees, lined by bracken and moss, and the odd flower growing in the shade. There were birds in the leaves overhead, and the branches occasionally bent under the weight of a passing squirrel. The woods were quite alive, with rustlings in the undergrowth and lots of deer tracks. 'I wonder if there are any real deer in the woods,' thought Charlotte. The path was getting deeper into the trees, climbing gently to the top of the hill. She was trying to think if the old house was on the other side, or at the bottom to her left when Roger came bounding over the underbrush, stopped right beside her and started barking at something she couldn't see. The trees became very still and she couldn't tell whether or not it was because of the dog's noise, or because of whatever it was he was barking at. A creeping fear began to get a hold of her, and her instinct was to turn and run out of the trees.

She remembered what the Green King had told her about fear, how it would spill over into the real world whenever it could. But what was causing it to happen? Was it her? She stopped, indecisive.

On the one hand she still wanted to go and see the house, on the other hand she didn't want to get grabbed and taken to the dark woods. She concentrated very hard on her own world. She looked at her watch. Ten past five. She concentrated on it. She had half an hour until she had to go home. Home. Charlotte concentrated very hard on home, and on not being afraid. She thought about her parents and her house, her favourite TV show, anything but the stillness of the trees. She reached a hand to her throat, felt the scarf and began to feel safer. Reassured, she walked on.

The path reached the top of the hill and then forked three ways. One branch went along the top of the hill, and presumably ended in the fields over town. Another one went over the top and she thought it might end near the river and the last one wound down to the left, back to the centre of the woods towards the clearing. She took the left fork, thinking that if it was the wrong one then at least she would end up somewhere familiar and she could come back and explore the other two later on.

Roger seemed to know where he was going, he dove onto a small rabbit track and bounded off into the undergrowth. His tail rose like a periscope over the bracken, meandering randomly over to each tree to sniff and lift a leg, back and forth, back and forth. About five minutes further, there was another path and Charlotte recognised it as the path to the house where she had fainted. She set off down the new track, whistling for Roger. She could see the house now, nestled in amongst the trees, silent and reassuring. It had withstood

89

fire, time, and the encroaching growth of the trees and stood there, a single roofless room, proof against decay.

As she got closer, Roger overtook her and raced ahead, diving into the house, and belatedly she wondered if Ken was in there, doing whatever it was he liked to do. No sign of him, however, and she walked through the space that used to be the door to be met by Roger, who promptly lay down and panted to himself.

She looked around. The air smelled the same as in the clearing, but it didn't feel as comfortable to her. What was left of the walls was grey stone, covered with a thin sheen of moss and lichen. There was grass growing inside, and a couple of scattered stones not quite big enough for seats.

Charlotte noticed lots of small, carved wooden figures in the old ruins, sitting in little niches in the wall where stones had fallen out. Lots and lots of them. Quite good most of them, too. There were dogs, rabbits, lots of deer, and a few human figures. Ken's work. 'This must be what he does in here,' she thought.

This house existed on both sides of the woods, she knew that much. She wondered if it were on the dark side, also. Frightened of what might happen if she tried to cross on her own she left the building and walked around the outside. 'It's not at all like the clearing in this part of the woods,' she thought. It was creepy.

She felt as if she was being watched by the walls, by the trees. 'Maybe I am,' she thought. Anyone could be watching her. The trees, the green people, even Ken or James could be hiding somewhere where she wouldn't see them. She looked around, hoping to see a deer, or a suspicious looking tree stump. No sign of the Green King anywhere. He'd hardly be looking for her every time she was in the woods – and besides, he was usually at the clearing, not here at all. Ken never saw him at all, and Ken spent his time here at the ruins. Still, she had the strongest feeling that there were eyes on her.

She started back towards the way out. She looked for the green people but nobody was around. Roger was sitting outside the house looking intently at all around, as if he felt something also.

She started feeling afraid. What if the ruined house went into all three woods? What if it were easier here for the dark woods to leak out? She didn't like this train of thought at all. She could feel the tendrils of fear again, stronger this time. She remembered what the Green King had told her, and she untied the material from around her neck and went to wrap it around her head.

Behind her, a twig cracked. Roger leapt to his feet, howling and barking. She turned around and what she saw froze her dead in her tracks. Coming across the ferns was a sheet of dark, slightly glowing mist. It flowed like water across the bracken, and behind it the bracken was dissolving into thickets of blackthorn. However, this blackthorn was without leaves and flowers, stout, gnarled branches covered in vicious looking two inch thorns.

Roger was already running down the path, she broke through her terror and careened after him, racing as fast as she could, forgetting everything she had been told by the Green King. She was too afraid to walk. She forgot everything except getting away from whatever was behind her. Roger had long disappeared. She was running faster than she ever had, her breath was coming in great rasping sobs and tears were starting to leak down her face, catching her flying hair in their moisture and plastering strands over her cheeks and lips.

She reached the fork in the path and shot right, downhill towards the clearing. She thought about the safety of the clearing, about how nice and light and safe it was in her part of the woods and began to feel better. Still she ran until she recognised the path and headed out of the woods, heart pounding, side aching. She hit a root, and fell down, twisting her ankle slightly, but not hurting it. As she stumbled back to her feet she risked a glance behind her. Nothing. The woods were quiet, but the birds were starting to sing again. She stopped. 'Stupid stupid stupid!' she told herself over and over. 'Stupid to go there, stupid to be afraid.'

It wasn't until she was at the top of the hill that she reached up to her head and noticed that the scarf was missing. She went back down the field and into the woods all the way to the turning that went up the hill but couldn't find it. Afraid to go up and back to the ruins, she ran out and climbed up to supper.

Helping her mother out with the chickens before supper, Charlotte was very silent.

"What's with you?" asked her mother. "You're very thoughtful..."

"Just thinking about what I'm going to do the rest of the summer, that's all. "

"That's not what's bothering you though, is it?" Charlotte's mother tried to cheer her up, but of course, she didn't know what was really troubling the girl and so nothing seemed to help.

At supper Charlotte's Dad noticed her mood also. "You're so glum. What's up? Summer's almost here, you've got weeks to explore and do whatever you want... This isn't like my girl at all," he added, with a slightly worried look at his daughter.

Charlotte secretly wished that they'd leave her alone. She finished supper and jumped up. "Can I go back outside for a while?"

Mrs. Enright studied her very carefully. "I think you should stay close to the house tonight," she said, "You're tired, I don't want you going too far."

Charlotte had a brainwave. "Can I go next door and visit Ken?" she asked. She'd never visited him at his house before, and she thought she could enlist his help in recovering the scarf.

Mrs. Enright smiled. "Of course you can, just as long as you don't go any further that his house."

So, Charlotte set off without Roger, walking up behind her house to Ken's place.

Chapter 8

It was seven thirty, and Charlotte had to be home by eight. If Ken was home there was just enough time to get into the woods and back. If he wasn't... Charlotte was trying to think of another plan.

The field separating the two houses was about a quarter of a mile wide. As she climbed the slope more and more of his house came into view.

First in sight came the chimneys she could see from her home, and then the rest of the house, surrounded by trees. It was a large, square old grey stone building with lots of windows, and a garage built separately from the rest of the house. There was a low wall around the grounds with a gate in it that was latched from the inside.

There was nobody in the garden to call to, so Charlotte had to walk all the way to the road and down the proper driveway. She thought about the 'other' house which, she realised, was probably how this house had looked before it had been changed by Ken's great grandfather. She thought about the old man and wondered if perhaps he was sitting right there in the garden as she approached.

She was surprised to hear the yapping of dogs greeting her as she approached. For some reason she had assumed that after Ken's dog had disappeared they hadn't got another one and she'd never seen him with another dog. A cat trotted across the pathway and into a clump of hydrangea bushes that were growing by the front door, which was inside a large square porch with windows and two steps up. She walked up and rang the doorbell rather nervously.

Mrs. Stone answered the door followed closely by three small white dogs, and invited her in immediately. Inside was a nice entrance room with a big coat closet, a couple of comfortable chairs - both of which were draped with cats - and a big staircase going upstairs.

"Charlotte! Fancy seeing you here! Lovely to see you, you should come more often. Come on in, I imagine you're here to see Ken, is that right? Get out of there you!" - this last to the dogs who were tripping over each other trying to smell Charlotte's shoes. Mrs. Stone was tall with dark hair and very pale skin. She was wearing a long blue summer dress and she smiled brightly at Charlotte.

"Yes, thank you Mrs. Stone," answered Charlotte crouching down to pat the dogs. As each one thrust a damp nose into her hands, Mrs. Stone turned around and yelled up the stairs.

"Ken! Ken... Charlotte's here to see you..."

A faint "Coming!" sounded from upstairs, and Mrs. Stone turned around.

"Just take a seat, scush the cats off the couch if you like. I'm so sorry, you've caught me right in the middle of my favourite show. Come and join us if you like, there's tea and biscuits."

"That's OK. Sorry to interrupt..." said Charlotte

"No no, I'm sorry to be so boring, it's just quite exciting at the moment and I can never work out the settings on the box to record things; Ken's the only one who can do that. Make yourself comfortable – sure you don't need anything?" she added, and swept out of the room followed by the dogs as Charlotte shook her head 'no'.

Charlotte stood uncomfortably for a minute or two, wishing she'd telephoned first – she realised she didn't even have a mobile number for Ken, or even knew if he had a phone. After a while she sat down on the edge of one of the chairs, being careful not to dislodge the cats that were lying there. There were animals everywhere, three cats in this room alone, plus the one outside, plus the three dogs... She wondered what else the house held.

Mrs. Stone came back in with a plate of biscuits for her and chatted for a few minutes in the commercial break, and then she heard footsteps on the top stairs, and Ken came around the corner and down to meet her.

"Allo," he said, "thought I'd be seeing you here one of these days." Not the best of starts, thought Charlotte. "What's up?" asked Ken.

"Um... it's..." now Charlotte was finally talking to him, she

94

had no idea quite how to phrase her problem. She decided to start at the beginning.

"I was in the woods, earlier... actually, I was exploring a bit and... well I ended up at that ruined house you took me to that day and I dropped ah, something, there."

Ken looked at her with a smile first, and then he seemed to understand. He got very serious. "Let me guess," he said, "you need me to come with you to get it, right?"

"Right," she said, relieved that he understood

"What exactly was it that you dropped?" he asked, frowning a little.

Charlotte looked at him, realized he'd think her a fool for what she had done.

"Well?"

"A scarf," she said in a small voice.

"A scarf. Just a scarf. Just any old scarf, or was it the scarf you were wearing the other day?"

"Um... yes." Charlotte felt more foolish at that moment than she had ever felt. She could feel Ken's eyes boring into her. She bit her lip for a second. "Oh, never mind. I'll just, I'll just go in and get it, I just, I thought maybe you'd understand," she rushed. She stopped, and as she was about to leave in a fluster of embarrassment and shame, Ken stopped her.

"'Um...yes' any old scarf or 'um...yes' the one you were wearing on Sunday?" he repeated, quite abruptly.

"I suppose it's 'um...yes the scarf I was wearing'," she said looking bashfully down at her feet. Ken's low snort through his nose sounded humorous and not very scornful so she looked back up. He was smiling and shaking his head.

"No, you're right," he sighed, "you can't go back in there by yourself. I think I can guess what happened. Do you know where you dropped it?"

"I think so. I was running away from the house and I went down the hill to the path that comes out below my house, and left the woods there. I went back and looked for it a bit, but I couldn't find it. I think it's on the path to the ruins."

"Well you picked a dandy place to lose it... It'll be safe

95

there though, no one ever goes in those woods anyway, and no animal will make off with it. The only thing that could possibly happen is that it gets picked up by whoever gave it to you." Ken paused significantly.

"I've got to be home by eight though..." Charlotte butted in.

"Well," said Ken thoughtfully, "then there's not enough time. It's seven thirty already. Can't it wait until tomorrow?"

"Seven thirty!" Charlotte was dismayed. It must have taken her longer than she thought to walk over, and Ken had taken forever to come down... She couldn't be late, her parents wouldn't let her out again after supper if she was late. "I don't want to leave it there all night..."

"There's another plan, of course," whispered, "ever been out to those woods at night?"

"Night?" asked Charlotte. Her heart began to beat a little harder. She thought quickly about the trees at night, and about how the night would swallow up that dark cloud so she wouldn't even be able to see it... "I don't know about that..."

"Oh don't be such a girl!" scoffed Ken. "Let's go outside. Bring the biscuits!"

The two of them went out and sat down on a bench in the Stones' garden. The scent of the evening wafted around them, cut grass from where Mr. Stone had just mowed their front lawn, roses, the clean air... It was all very pleasant. Not at all like... Charlotte stopped herself, aware of what had happened the last time she'd thought fearfully of those dark woods.

The plan they came up with was as follows: Charlotte's parents were usually asleep by eleven. Ken's parents stayed up later but once he was in bed they never disturbed him. Underneath his window was a shed that he could climb onto to get in and out of the house. He was going to arrive at her house at midnight and throw dirt at her window, then she would creep downstairs meet him. If her parents woke up she was going to tell them she was going downstairs for a drink of juice - she'd stay in her pyjamas until she got outside. All she had to do was stash clothing and a torch somewhere.

The only problem was Roger and Charlotte decided she'd keep him in her room until she left so he wouldn't wake up her parents. If he barked when she got home she would just say she'd woken him up getting a drink.

All the way home, Charlotte's mind was whirling. She was both terrified and excited at the same time. Once home she went upstairs, grabbed her oldest jeans and a jumper, her torch and penknife and shoved them into a bag which she snuck out and hid behind the house.

She almost gave the game away by being too excited but her parents were just happy to see her in good spirits again and not moping around. Privately they thought it had something to do with Ken, and they didn't really notice how agitated she really was.

After her bedroom lights were out there was no way Charlotte was going to sleep. She lay in bed going over and over the route to the ruins, which was the best way to go in, and where she thought she had dropped the scarf. Then she told herself over and over not to think about the Green King when she was out in the woods, just to think about school the next day, her parents, anything that would stop her from accidentally crossing over and triggering a hole through which the dark fog would leak.

She decided to tell Ken about the old man in his house - she felt it was important for him to know, and she owed him one for the favour he was doing her. It would mean telling him all about the other world, but she had a feeling Ken knew more than he was telling, anyway.

At about quarter past ten she heard her parents climb the stairs and potter about getting ready for bed. The familiar sounds of them going in and out of the bathroom to brush their teeth almost lulled her to sleep, but then she'd remember and jerk herself awake again. She heard Roger padding down the hallway to her room as usual, and she crept out of bed and opened the door to let him in.

Once the house was quiet and Roger asleep on the carpet by her bed, Charlotte found it harder and harder to stay

97

awake. She got out of bed and sat on the windowsill and looked out across at the trees, just visible in the rising moon.

In there. In there somewhere. The scarf was very important, this she knew, and it was in there, somewhere. What a fool she was to have dropped it, what an idiot. She cursed herself over and over again...

The dirt hit the window beside her ear and she jerked awake. Roger also woke up with a quiet 'whoof', and Charlotte shushed him gently; he settled down and went back to sleep. She peered through the window and could make out Ken standing beside the house in the moonlight.

It was a very bright moon which would be full in a day or two. It hung over the trees and cast a silver glow over the whole countryside. She waved down, and from where he was standing Ken saw her disappear. He waited for a couple of minutes, worried, and then he heard her footsteps on the grass.

"I almost forgot my shoes," she explained. She continued on around the back and grabbed her bag. She was about to climb into her outdoor clothes when Ken motioned her to follow him.

"Not here, the dog'll hear us and start barking," he whispered.

They walked down to the wall at the foot of the garden, climbed the gate and on the other side Charlotte pulled her clothes over her pyjamas and stashed her bag in the bushes.

"Now. Got everything?" asked Ken.

"Yes, and I bought my penknife...just in case," she added as she sensed Ken looking at her funny.

Ken was wondering if this was such a good idea after all. He did know the danger of being in the woods at night and was worried that Charlotte would slow things down. 'Still', he thought, 'she's not just any girl, she can run fast, and she knows what's going on.' Maybe more than he himself, he thought wryly.

They set off down the field to the pathway that Charlotte used.

"Can you really not remember where you had it last?"

asked Ken, for about the fourth time. "Think..."

"I was about to knot it around my head when I... um... started to run... I thought I was holding onto it... I fell down at the bottom of the hill but I went back there afterwards and looked and I couldn't find it."

"Did you leave the path?"

"No..." Charlotte was silent a moment. "No, I didn't." She looked over at Ken. In the moonlight she could see the boy was quite distinctly beside her, in fact, it looked almost as if he was glowing slightly. She looked closer, and realized that there was a slight glow coming from him, almost imperceptible.

In fact, it was coming from his shirt. She reached over a tentative hand and brushed the fabric at the hem. It was soft under her hand. Ken was looking at her as they walked, not saying anything.

"Want to know how I got it?" he asked.

"Sure," she said, and then shut up. Getting Ken to talk about anything was rare enough, getting him to talk about the woods was impossible, and this, surely, had to do with the woods.

"My Great-grandfather had a trunk of things he kept in the attic. When he died it just got left there. One day my mother went through it. There was quite a bit of this fabric and when I was little I used to have a blanket made out of it. I really liked it and later she made me a couple of these shirts out of it. I was really young but she made them big or something."

"What about the rest of the fabric?" she asked.

"Dunno. I think it's still in the trunk. Most of the stuff was pretty useless, just memorabilia. I got some other things, though. Got this," he said, and bent down. He was wearing his usual walking boots, and out of the right one he drew a knife, an old hunting knife. The blade gleamed dimly in the light. "It's got a blackthorn handle with a coat of arms on it. I got it when I turned thirteen as a present. I always have them in the woods, the knife and the shirt. I feel, I dunno, unprotected without them."

"Does your shirt always do that in the dark?" she asked

99

him, looking at the glow.

"Yep. When there's no moon at all it gets brighter, it's quite dim right now because the moon's almost full. We should be able to spot your scarf easily - it is made out of the same stuff, isn't it..."

"Mine's greener though," added Charlotte.

"It'll probably fade with time."

They had reached the path and were making their way into the trees. There were vague rustlings in the undergrowth as the nocturnal animals foraged for food. Once, something swooped out of the air and the wind of its passing moved through their hair. Charlotte jumped a little.

"Owl," explained Ken.

"How do you know it's not a bat or something?" asked Charlotte.

"Bats don't make that much wind, besides they prefer it by the river where all the insects are. There's quite a few owls in here, sometimes you can surprise them sleeping in the day."

"Oh," said Charlotte, not feeling very much better.

They were looking for anything that glowed, and then turning on their torches and looking again, just in case.

"I've already looked along here," offered Charlotte.

"Doesn't hurt to look again," said Ken, shortly. They were talking in low voices, although there wasn't any real need. The woods were quite dark, not much light filtered down through the trees at all. The trees loomed comfortingly around them, and for the moment Charlotte wasn't nervous at all.

Ken was enjoying himself. He loved the woods at night, this wasn't the first time he'd let himself down onto the shed outside his window and gone for a late night ramble. There was total peace, no chance of some townsman walking his dog and disturbing things, and a multitude of nocturnal animals to observe. There was a badger burrow near the edge of the woods and along the top there were foxes. There were rabbits along the hedgerows closer to his house and they loved to come out at night. There were voles and field mice, all sorts of animals that preferred to go about under the safe cover of the dark.

Ken also knew something he thought Charlotte didn't. Just after he had seen James in the clearing with the Green people all those years ago, he had also seen the glowing fog for the first time. It was at night, and all he'd seen was a glowing wave moving slowly through the underbrush. It had moved out in a circle like spilled water from a point about a hundred feet away, and he hadn't hung around to see what it did. He'd seen it other times also, by day. He didn't know what it was, or what caused it, but he knew that it scared him down to his toes. He hadn't had to ask Charlotte what made her run, and knowing that she'd seen the fog too made him feel even friendlier towards her. He was keeping an eye out for it at all times.

They reached the turn in the path, and the place where Charlotte had fallen. No sign of the scarf. They started up the hill in companionable silence, waving their lights, Charlotte itching to ask Ken more questions. Questions like: where did he think his great-grandfather had got the cloth?

To her surprise, Ken asked the first question. "So, how did you get up on that stag?"

"I knew you were going to ask that," she said, and then promptly shut up. 'Make him stew for a change,' she thought.

"Well?" he asked. "Let me guess," his voice dripping with sarcasm. "That stag just walked up to you, kneeled down and said 'get on', right?"

"Right!" she laughed, knowing it would annoy him.

"No, seriously!" Ken protested.

"Seriously, that's exactly what happened!" said Charlotte, and she couldn't keep the smile out of her voice.

"Look!" said Ken, becoming a little angry. "I'll level with you about anything you want to know, I'm being serious here. Didn't I come all the way over to your house at midnight to help you look for your stupid scarf, didn't I..." he was beginning to splutter, and Charlotte interrupted him, laughing.

"Calm down, come on, I really am telling you the truth."

Ken stopped, exasperated. He was tiring of this game, and only the fact that he had actually seen her with his own eyes riding on the animal's back stopped him from storming off home. She knew something, and he wanted to know exactly what.

"Come on," she said, "you really want to know, and I'm telling you the truth. Remember what you said about that time you found James way back when he was missing? About the people turning into deer?"

"Yes... oh," said Ken, making the connection.

Charlotte cast around with her torch, saw no sign of her scarf and they resumed climbing in silence again. She cleared her throat. "Something else happened too..."

"What?" asked Ken, turning on his torch briefly.

Charlotte told Ken about finding the old man living in his house in the other world. She explained all about what had happened, and how she had crossed over. Ken didn't seem too surprised, just frustrated.

"I've been able to see things sometimes, you know, things that aren't there, really. I've seen the old man at the house before, I thought he was a ghost. He frightened me half to death when I was a kid, but my mother told me he was a friendly ghost and not to worry."

"I've seen people in the woods sometimes, too. I've often wondered if there was another world, but I've never been able to GET there for some reason." He sighed and Charlotte could see through the darkness that he was shaking his head. "And then," he continued "then you come along and waltz right in..."

"Sorry," said Charlotte.

"I just wish I knew more about it," said Ken. "It all seems so... I don't know. Familiar? Maybe I'm crazy."

"Maybe we both are," Charlotte agreed with a chuckle. They reached the last turnoff to the ruins without having seen any sign of the scarf.

Charlotte was loath to follow the pathway again. All she could think of was what had happened last time. Certain that her fear had caused it to grow in strength before, she wanted to be certain she was safe. Ken sensed her trepidation, and reached over and took her hand which made her feel instantly better and safer.

They walked slowly, first looking for the glow, and then again with the lights turned on. They were looking under leaves and plants in case it had been thrown underneath the ferns in her flight.

About halfway between the junction of the two paths and the house itself, Charlotte saw a glow, about ten feet away from the path.

"Ken!" she said, quite loudly. He jumped a bit, he was tense also. "There it is, see?" She let go his hand and started towards it.

Ken looked. He saw Charlotte leave the path and head towards the glow. As she picked her way through the bracken he wondered idly how on earth the scarf had gotten so far from the path, and then realized that the glow was bright, too bright, and it was getting brighter. He saw Charlotte stop a few feet away and the hairs on the back of his neck rose as she turned around and leapt away, screaming "RUN, Ken, RUN!!!!"

He saw the glow burst into the fog that had stalked his dreams for years, he saw it overtake her, and before he could reach her it had overtaken him, too, and raced outwards leaving behind it a tangle of thorns and deadwood. He leapt towards Charlotte to grab her, thorns tearing at his jeans. Just as he reached her she faded away clear into nothing, along with the thorns, and he was left standing alone in the familiar woods at night, calling "Charlotte! Charlotte!" over and over again.

At his feet he saw a dim glow, and bent down. There indeed was the scarf. He picked it up, wound it into a rope and tied it around his neck.

Chapter 9

Charlotte stood in the thicket of thorns looking at the place where Ken had been standing and blinked. She looked around frantically, but nothing looked familiar except the path, ten feet away.

She knew at once what had happened. She had somehow been caught by the other side, and was in the dark woods, alone, at night. She struggled against the thorns, panic stricken, but the more she struggled, the more the thorns tangled in her clothing, ripping it to shreds and holding her still. After two or three endless minutes she realized the bushes weren't actually moving, and that if she stood still, she was alright.

She tried to remember exactly what it was that the Green King had told her.

'Calm down, Charlotte!' she told herself, but the vision of the Green King saying "Stay on the paths, get out of the woods," kept replaying in her head, over and over again.

The path wound innocently through the thickets of dead trees, so close, but yet so far. Every time she bent to untangle the thorns, another piece of her clothing caught and she became even more trapped. She was bleeding from cuts in her hands and arms, and one on her right leg where the thorns had ripped through both her jeans and her pyjamas underneath. The thorns had worked their way all the way up to her shoulders, and she was trapped. Her heart was pounding in fear, she was gasping for breath even though she wasn't moving at all.

Concentrate on home, she thought to herself. She stood very still, and thought hard about her house. She tried hard not to be afraid. 'There's nothing to fear but fear itself,' she repeated. 'It's just trying to scare me, it can't hurt me...' She thought about her parents, her bedroom, 'Concentrate, Charlotte, concentrate... I feel like Dorothy in *The Wizard of Oz* shouting, "There's no place like home!" Only wish I had a magic pair of red shoes...' she thought wistfully. With this thought, a few of the thorns relinquished their hold.

It's working! She thought about her favourite movies, her school, anything she could imagine. She stood for ages and ages, but no matter how hard she concentrated, the thorns would only loosen, and not disappear.

'I'm too weak!' she cried to herself. The Green King had warned her that she was not strong enough yet. Although, she remembered, she had been strong enough to cross into the bright world by herself – not once, but twice. So, she ought to be able to... She concentrated. Use something from your own world, he had said. Her clothes? They were in shreds. She wasn't wearing any jewellery and she had dropped her torch, it was still lit but sitting by her left foot and impossible to reach. Her trainers!

Her feet were wrapped in thorns and tendrils of undergrowth, impossible to reach without ripping her face on the way. She tried for five minutes to concentrate on the feel of her shoes on her feet, the rubber soles, and the manmade fabric. The thorns kept relaxing but still would not let go, and the woods refused to fade away.

She remembered her penknife. It was in the back pocket of her jeans. Her right hand was fairly free of thorns, and she started easing it down to her pocket. Every tremor she made caused the thorns to embed themselves deeper in her clothing. She tried moving slower and slower, and eventually found a speed slow enough to fool the bushes.

Almost half an hour passed. Her hand was close to her knife, but her pocket was covered with thorns. She was exhausted from trying to stand still. Her left leg was almost completely asleep from the position in which she was standing. She felt dizzy and nauseous, tired, and dreadfully, dreadfully afraid.

She wondered what would happen if she wasn't home in the morning when her parents got up, and then remembered Ken. He would either be going for help or trying to find her. She rather hoped he had gone home, she didn't want her parents woken up in the middle of the night. Maybe he could contact the Green... Then she remembered that the Green King couldn't come and get her even if he knew where she was.

With this last thought, her knees started to give way. She sagged a little and the thorns dug in even further. When she tried to straighten up, they tightened more, and several pierced through her clothes and dug into her skin.

She screamed, and jumped, and the bushes gave a sudden tug. She felt herself being dragged to the forest floor, and she landed sitting up with her right foot underneath her, painfully twisted, cocooned in thorny branches. She gave herself up to tears.

It had taken Ken a while to realize that it was probably his shirt that had saved him from the fog. He almost took it off then and there before he figured out that it was better if one of them were on the right side, than both of them on the wrong with no way out. He searched for a while more before he walked purposefully into the ruins of the old warden's house.

James was asleep. Sound asleep. He was dreaming a dream he hadn't had since he was very, very young. In the dream he was sitting beside his bedroom window and there was the Green King standing outside, just like old times. The King was waving to him Come down... Come down...

The dream faded, and James woke up slowly. He stretched with his eyes closed, and then opened them slowly, expecting the light of morning to greet him. Instead, the room was dark.

Befuddled, he rolled over and turned on the light. The clock on his wall said that it was 01:35; he'd only been asleep about three hours. He turned the light off again, and tried to get back to sleep, unsuccessfully. Every time he closed his eyes he could see that man... So familiar... He just couldn't quite place him...

James sat bolt upright, now fully awake. With chills running down his spine he got out of bed and looked out of

106

the window. His heart skipped a beat. Standing in the moonlight was the Green King, with four or five others like him. They didn't move, just stood staring up at his window.

'James, we need you. Come down, James...' the voices rang in his head.

James didn't need any further encouraging. He waved once and thought 'Coming!' and began to put on thick long underwear, his thickest shirt and heavy canvas workpants... his cave clothes. 'Why now?' he thought, but only to himself.

In her sleep in her home on the other side of the woods, Rosemary moaned and rolled over, waking up her sister in the bed across the room.

Roger twitched and whoofed but didn't wake up from his forbidden sleep on Charlotte's empty bed.

The Green People were moving. The hills were alive with deer, stationed at all the exits from the woods, waiting, hoping. The word had gone out from the Watcher that something was happening.

The Lady stood in the clearing, gathering her power, her enormous strength for the battle ahead.

Charlotte was singing. Under her breath she was singing a nursery rhyme, trying anything she could to remind herself of home and to stay awake. Her chin was dropped to her chest, and she was sagging forward. Only the thorns in her shirt stopped her from collapsing face first. Her foot underneath her was numb. Her whole body was numb. She felt calm, not afraid at all. She just wanted to sleep, sleep right where she was...

Where was she again? She couldn't quite remember. That's

right. She was in the woods, in the clearing in the bright woods... She saw herself sitting in the clearing with Roger and Ken and the Lady... They were talking. Actually, the Lady was talking, but she couldn't hear her, it was just a buzzing sound.... bxzzzbdzzzz... the Lady was really trying to make her understand something...

The Lady was trying very hard in fact. In the bright woods she was standing in the clearing trying to send her mind where her body could not go. "What's happening to her?" Ken asked anxiously. "Why doesn't she cross over?"

"The thorns are stopping her!" the Lady cried. "Each thorn has a hollow end, filled with a slow acting poison. Unless Charlotte leaves the thorns and goes onto the path right away, she'll die in the dark woods. And we could all die in the green woods!"

"How could that happen?" Ken asked, alarmed. He knew the green woods were connected to the 'real' world, but even so... Why were the Green people so frantic?

"The night is awake. The dark woods are taking a form of their own. They have gathered strength for years, and are finally achieving self-awareness. With consciousness comes the desire for physical form, and it needs something to give it that form... The move has been made in a game that might change the balance of power in the woods, and across the whole world..." the Lady declared ominously. "These woods have been around for a very, very long time. Longer than recorded history... They are the remnants of some of the very first woods and they are, together with a few other patches of trees of all kinds that are scattered around Britain and the rest of the world, places of power, where Nature still rules."

"But there has been talk in the 'real' world, of tearing down parts of these woods, making more land for housing and parks. The town wants to turn most of the area into a manicured showground, with picnic areas, playing fields - tear down acres and acres of the trees and build a new town

108

hall, a nice, urban area, controlled, clean! People say the woods are dangerous. That the trees are old, useless. They say that the town is still growing, and needs more land. With most of the surrounding area being vital farmland, the only land left for redevelopment is the woods and some marshland - and the town wants it all!"

"Even as I speak, there's a study being done by City Hall comparing the cost of draining the marshes versus the cost of chopping down the trees and selling the wood. With another child missing in the woods, the town will certainly decide in favour of razing the woods!"

James was also in the woods. He was standing beside the dead tree stump, listening. The stump towered over him in the dark. Behind him, hidden under the climbing ivy was a small hole, just big enough for a man to squeeze through. This was the entrance to the caves.

This was the stump Charlotte had seen. James had discovered it as a child and spent many an afternoon wandering inside the caves with a ball of string to help him find his way back. He wasn't afraid of it, or of the things inside it. In fact, part of James understood them, their dark need to destroy... A part of James even, in fact, felt drawn to them.

The original ball of string had long since rotted away, but James no longer needed it. He knew the caves well, had found many interesting things there, including two skeletons, one an enormous man and very, very old, and the other one obviously a child, probably one of the missing ones. He had never told anyone about them, he didn't want anyone else to know about the caves at all.

The caves were the mirror image of the woods. Where the clearing was open and sunny, they were enclosed and dark. Where the clearing was the central point of power for the bright woods, the caves were the same for the dark. And James had seen the dark woods. James had been into the dark woods. James knew the dark woods just as Ken knew the light.

It was through these caves that James could enter the dark woods easiest. He had been walking in there many times. He knew what would happen if the thorns caught him because there were more bones in the woods than he could count, all of them wrapped in thorns somewhere off the path.

The dark woods didn't scare James at all. They were his, all his, and he knew them as well as he knew the woods in the real world. He had found them one afternoon just before he had gotten lost as a child. Climbing on the stump he had fallen and rolled part of the way into the main entrance, which had been obscured by years of ivy growth and ferns. He had gotten a ball of string from the farm's workshop, and, remembering the old Greek myth of the Minotaur's maze, had tied one end to an ivy vine at the entrance and started exploring.

The caves went down quite steeply for a while and then wandered for what seemed like miles. James thought they probably went underneath the whole woods, perhaps even under the river and into the town. There were a couple of exits that he knew of, and he suspected there were holes that reached the surface all through the area, as the air was always quite fresh.

Down at the centre of the cave system James had found a large cavern, had gotten frightened and run out of the caves in terror to find himself in the dark woods. He hadn't realized his fear had caused him to cross over, and had gone back inside the caves hunting for a door back into his own world. He had found his dropped ball of string, calmed down, and found his way out safely.

The first time he'd been taken by the fog it was a sunny afternoon and he'd brought his fishing rod down to the river. He was sitting a few feet away from a path, daydreaming about the dark woods, not realizing the effect his thoughts would have. The fog had exploded silently and left him surrounded by the thorns. He'd have been wrapped up like Charlotte if it hadn't been for the river close by. Riverbed, actually, for there was no water running there. There seemed

110

to be no water in the dark land, or very little. He had wrenched free of the thorns and leapt into the dry bed close by, walked along to the nearest path and then home via the caves, feeling woozy and nursing his wounds.

He had tried to trigger the fog by himself again, but it was difficult, as he didn't feel frightened very often. James was made of sterner stuff than most people. Over time he had figured out how to get in and out easily, but it was always easier when he started from the cavern, just as it was easier for Charlotte to cross over through the clearing.

For years, James had had no idea what exactly the dark woods were. He knew it was dangerous in there and he'd seen some of the things that walked around. They looked human, but they were darker, faster. He had seen one of them take a fox once that was obviously lost – it was horrible. After that he gave the monsters an even wider berth. They were easy to see coming and they didn't know about the caves. Plus, he realised that if he stayed calm, they ignored him.

The calm in the dark woods made him feel better, there were few birds, almost no wind, almost total silence. The fear didn't bother him. He had liked the thrill of walking so close to danger, and while he didn't go very often anymore, he visited once in a while to trim the paths.

Now, he knew a lot about the dark world. He'd seen it leak out, seen it lurking around the cave mouth. The minds of people triggered it to come. Minds full of fear, full of hate would cause it to swirl and eddy out of thin air, although people who were concerned too much with the real world wouldn't bother it at all. These people couldn't cross into the bright woods either, though.

James knew that Charlotte was lost in the dark woods. He spent a few minutes trying to conjure the woods into being, but couldn't seem to manage it: something was stopping him. He knew it would be easier to start from the cavern, and so he started on the long climb down.

Ken was sitting in the ruins. He was sprawled on the ground with his head pillowed against one of the rocks lying there, and to a stranger, he would have appeared to be sleeping.

There were green people at all the gates out of the woods, looking to a casual observer like deer grazing in the moonlight. As soon as something happened in the real world they were ready to jump if they were needed. They waited.

The sun was coming up. The Lady had told Ken that Charlotte could only last another four and a half hours before the slow poison would stop her heart... Her parents still slept, unaware of the peril their daughter was in.

Across the fields, the Starlings were beginning to wake up.

"Ted!" called Mrs. Starling to her eldest son, "Would you go and roust your brother out of bed, the lazy sod?"

Young Ted sighed and started up the stairs.

The Stones slept, since they, like Charlotte's parents, wouldn't be getting up until seven.

James was standing in the dark woods. It had been harder than usual to cross over. The wan, yellowy-brown light that leaked through seemed the same. It never got any brighter or darker than this, the sky always seemed to be overcast, but it never rained.

The trees were bony. They had no leaves, or even any bark – their trunks were smooth. Termites lived in them, chewing them into dust. Once in a while one would fall. James had wondered what would happen when all the trees were fallen, but had stopped when he realized that some of the saplings that seemed to be dead were slowly getting taller every year.

Things grew in this land, but in very strange ways.

James started off on the path that circled the trees and headed in the direction that the green people had told him to go, all the time looking beside the path for Charlotte.

112

Back in the 'real' world, young Ted had discovered that James was already up, and the Starlings assumed he was either in the woods or doing his chores already, and didn't give him a second thought.

"Just so long as he's back in time for school," said old Ted.

In the bright woods, things were still. The trees were silent for once, and everyone not stationed outside the woods was gathered in the clearing. The Lady raised her arms, and tried again to reach Charlotte with her mind. She sent a burst of energy, as much as she could get through the 'real' world and into the dark world.

In the thorns, Charlotte felt a stinging feeling on her face. It seemed to wake her up a little. She felt less groggy... She tried to lift up her head. Again, a stinging feeling, like a slap, hit her cheeks. She opened up her eyes. She saw the thorns.

She had a terrible headache and everything hurt. She could feel thorns scratching at her everywhere and most of her clothes were torn. She looked down at her legs. The hems of both her jeans and her pyjamas were torn to ribbons and the ribbons were slowly turning to dust. Her pocket knife was sitting on the earth to one side of her, since the pocket had crumbled away. As she bent down to try again to pick up her knife, she realized that under the branches the stems grew straight for a couple of feet up – there was a tunnel beneath the tangles of thorns.

She still felt dizzy, but with her sleeves rotted away and the help from the Lady, she could move just enough to reach her knife without disturbing the bushes. She inched her hand towards it, grabbed it and opened it slowly. Feeling how solid it was, feeling the metal blade helped her concentrate on getting the thorns to relax their grip.

James walked along the paths. There was nothing different so far, the old bones lay still, slowly turning to dust, nothing new. "Anyone there?" he whispered just in case, remembering the patrolling monsters. There was no answer. He reached the path up the hill and began to trot a little.

As he reached the top he thought he could hear something. Hearing anything in these silent woods was uncommon, and instinctively he turned towards the sound. It appeared to be coming from the direction of the old ruined house and he hurried up to the junction of the paths. Turning towards the ruins, he heard someone crying out for help in a weak voice. He started to run down the path, mindful of the thorns hanging over it, and finally saw Charlotte, her head just visible in the bushes.

The girl was grey, her skin hung flaccid from her face, she looked like an old woman. Her clothes were tattered, and her face was bent back towards the sky. She saw James, and called out to him in relief.

"James, James, thank God you're here..." she was laughing and crying at the same time, trying to keep as still as possible.

"We've got to be quiet!" he said. "Don't make too much noise... you don't want to attract them."

"Who?" cried Charlotte, suddenly more afraid than before, as if that were possible.

"Them!" answered James in a whisper. He sat down on the path as close to her as possible and tried to concentrate on bringing the real world back into existence around them. It was a vague hope, but it might work. He concentrated, but it was no good. They had to get to the caves.

"Ohh... just get me out of here... I don't think I can stand this any longer," sobbed the girl.

James thought for a second. "Concentrate on your house or something - that could help loosen the thorns?"

"I've been TRYING!" she said. "I've got my penknife but they've only loosened... And I'm so tired..." she trailed off. "If I can get to the ground I think I can crawl under the bushes."

"Good idea – just hurry, we have to get to the caves."

"Don't go without me!" she pleaded.

"I won't," he promised, but he knew that if one of them came, he would leave her in a second. The Green King knew this too, knew that James' greatest strength, his lack of fear, made him ruthless.

She closed her eyes, again felt her knife solid in her fingers. With James there it was easier for her to concentrate on her own world, and the thorns started to give way. One by one they sprang back over her head, and she found herself underneath a deadly canopy, in a tunnel of trunks through which she could see the path, tantalizingly close. She grabbed her torch and tried to move. She eased herself onto her hands and knees, screaming in pain as she moved her injured ankle. Her legs began to burn with pins and needles.

"You O.K.?" asked James.

"I... think so," she answered. "I think I've hurt my ankle."

"Try and crawl between the stems. I'll help you if I can," said James.

Charlotte wondered how long she'd been in the thorns. She could see the light coming through the trees, a pale, watery light filtering through the thorns. She could feel the fear tugging at her heart, at her muscles, she wanted to run, to bolt, but she had to crawl slowly and carefully through the stems, her knees sinking slightly into dry and dusty ground underneath.

Finally, she reached James's hand, and with his help pulled herself onto the path, and lay there, feeling both elated and terrified, with her body waking up in painful bits and pieces.

She thought she heard a roar, muted and far away, sounding between the trees. She looked at James; he'd obviously heard it too.

"What was that?"

James looked at her, and then over to where the sound had started. "I think it was by the river. They like it there for some reason. Thankfully, it's far away. We have to get to the caves," he repeated. "How's that ankle?"

115

"Fine. How are we going to get back?"

"Easy. If we can't cross back right here, I'll get us to the caves. Just concentrate on getting home, and I'll give it a try."

James looked into the trees and thought hard about his home. Nothing happened. He concentrated harder, and thought he may be having success. Charlotte yelled at him.

"James! Don't leave me behind! James!"

He looked around and realized that Charlotte and the Dark woods were fading out. She wasn't able to cross with him – must be something to do with the poison the thorns had given her. He stopped crossing back and stood in the Dark woods.

Charlotte looked up at him. He was crouched over her with his hair in his eyes and a worried expression on his face. "James," she said, as firmly as she could. "Let's just get out of here, we can look at my ankle later."

James smiled for a second. "Alright then," he said, and they started off.

There was another roar from across the woods, this time sounding as if it came from closer, from just over the hill.

James leapt to his feet. "Come on, we've got to get moving!" He helped Charlotte stand up. Her pins and needles were almost gone, but her right ankle was swollen and painful.

"Where are these caves?" asked Charlotte as they stumbled down the path, James supporting her.

"They're by this old root that's down at the bottom of the hill, on the way to the farm."

Charlotte remembered the gloomy old tree stump and shivered. The old root seemed to be so far away... "I was told to get out of the woods if I got stuck in here," she announced.

James looked at her in surprise. "Who told you that?"

"The Green King," she said, tired of keeping him secret.

"The Green King?" James pondered this for a moment as they struggled on. They reached the T-junction and started off down the hill. "Well, he didn't tell me that, and I've been

116

in these woods more than anyone living, I expect. I'm just supposed to get you out and I can't do that unless I go to the caves, so that's that."

"You've seen him today?" Charlotte was ecstatic. She looked at James briefly, then they stumbled.

"Keep yer eyes on the path!" he grunted.

They heard another roar, coming from a different direction. It was answered by whatever was behind them, still quite far off.

"They may not know where we are, but we've gotta hurry," panted James in a low voice. "Here, can't you go any faster?"

At the note of panic in his voice, Charlotte tried to run a little faster, landed on her ankle and fell, painfully. She let out a little squeak. James reached down and hoisted her into the air like a bale of hay. He stood her on her feet and motioned for her to climb onto his back, and the two of them lurched forward to the bottom of the hill.

It only took a minute to get to the path to the stump, but it seemed like it took forever. They could hear grunts and moans from behind them.

"We've got to be quiet," James murmured over his shoulder. "If they hear us they'll come running over," he panted, "and they're fast".

"What are they?" muttered Charlotte into his ear.

"Tell you later," he gasped as they rounded the corner and headed for the stump.

"We've got to get out of the woods, this path reaches the edge quicker than it does the stump," urged Charlotte. James kept running, he could see the path to the stump, and he was still undecided.

They were almost at the turn when the first of the things spotted them. It came running from the edge of the wood, and their route was decided. Charlotte gasped. It was like looking at a real life cartoon of a human being. Its face was human, but its skin was dark and sagging, almost black. Its eyes were almost covered by sagging skin, its teeth were bared, and sharp. It was naked, but the skin on its body hung

117

like sacks and ropes so it looked like it was wearing a tattered leather coat. Its hands were held in front of it and the nails were sharp as claws. It was running quite fast, and James was loaded down.

Even James hadn't seen one that close before, and he felt a burst of extra adrenalin in his system. They rushed down to the bottom of the valley, where they could see the stump sitting. The grunts from behind them told them that there were now two of the things following them. Charlotte risked a glance over her shoulder. The things had stopped for a second and seemed to be fighting, giving James just the time he needed to reach the stump.

Charlotte tumbled off his back, and he dragged her through the entrance to the cave. On the way in Charlotte hit a thorn bush, and it instantly came to life, the branches filling the entranceway, one of them hooked into the remains of her jeans. She was about to scream in fear when the already weak fabric gave way, and she was left with another hole in her jeans, but her skin intact.

With the entranceway blocked by the thorns, the things couldn't get in, but neither could James and Charlotte get out. The monstrous forms patrolled the entrance, but seemed to be as afraid of the thorns as they were. Feeling safer, Charlotte collapsed in exhaustion against the wall.

James was fishing about in the dark for something. Suddenly a light appeared from his corner: he had found his torch. Charlotte turned hers on also; it shone briefly and then flickered out. "I've got spare batteries if it takes 'C' cells," called James from his corner.

"Two of them," replied Charlotte, surprised. James threw her a packet of batteries. His cache had several things in it, including a canteen of water, which he offered her. She hadn't thought about it until he offered, but she was incredibly thirsty. She took a sip. It was a bit stale and brackish, but it made her feel a lot better.

A low grumbling sound filtered up from the caves below. The two of them looked at each other. There was no turning back, they had to go forward. Charlotte closed the canteen, opened her penknife and gripped it fearfully.

The caves were dry, dusty even, like everything else in this world. There were fallen rocks, grey and dull. No interesting formations, nothing, just grey rock, going down into the earth.

"There's lots of passageways in these caves," said James. "I know them pretty well. We're going to make our way down to the main cavern and try to get out from there by concentrating. It's the easiest point in the woods. Otherwise there's an exit that comes out by the bridge and we can try and get out there."

"How many exits are there?" asked Charlotte.

"Two others that I've found," answered James, helping her over some fallen rocks. "One's by the bridge, the other is by that ruined house, but there was a rock fall there two years ago and you can't get out, otherwise we'd have gone in that way in the first place."

Charlotte's heart sank. If they couldn't get out in the cavern, they were going to have to wander around in the dark with whatever it was that was down there making the noise and then walk all the way across the woods to the bridge. Her ankle throbbed painfully, and her heart pounded in her ears.

The sounds of the things outside the entrance began to fade as they descended deeper into the earth, and the grumbling from below gradually increased in loudness.

The two of them kept close together, stopping at every cross-tunnel to listen. The sounds seemed to be coming from directly in front of them, from inside the cavern...

Chapter 10

Back at Charlotte's house, the alarm clocks were going off. It was Friday morning, and Mr. Enright was getting ready for work. He didn't look in on his daughter, and it wasn't for another twenty minutes that her mother found the empty room, about the same time Mrs. Stone discovered that Ken was missing, too. Ken's mother started preparing breakfast, certain he was just up early and walking around outside.

Mrs. Enright was more curious. Roger had been let out at his usual time, and was sitting under the chestnut tree, whining ever so slightly, looking at the trees.

She called for her daughter. No answer. She called louder. Still no answer. She was annoyed. Charlotte had left no note, and it was unlike her to disappear without the dog. On impulse, she went to the phone and called Mrs. Stone.

Ken was still in the ruins, but now he was out of his trance. What had happened to him was this: after Charlotte had disappeared he had started to run down to the clearing on impulse to see if he could find the Green King, when something tripped him and he lost consciousness. When he came to, he was staring the Green King in the face. He thought he must be dreaming, he'd never seen him up close before. He was beautiful – old but not old, ageless almost. He glowed slightly and when Ken looked closely he realised that the man's skin wasn't completely green, it was a slowly swirling mix of all colours that looked like green from far away. He blinked and looked around, and he realised that light was beginning to filter through the sky.

"Oh my God! What time is it?"

"It's nearly dawn. We felt a commotion in the woods a few hours ago and a patrol just found you – it looks like you were caught by the other side but it couldn't quite catch you. Look," said the Green King, pointing to Ken's trouser leg. The fabric was torn to shreds, and a deep scratch marked his leg. A small piece of thorn was lodged in a scrap of fabric. "It looks as though your shirt saved you – your mother might know more than she lets on."

Ken's head was in a whirl – how did the Green King know about his shirt? About his Mother? What was going on? Then it came back to him and he cried: "Charlotte's caught on the wrong side of the woods – she was with me."

"What?" The Green King looked startled. "What was she doing in the woods at night? How did it happen?" He was serious and a wave of terrifying energy came from him. "STUPID girl, I gave her something…" he reached out and tugged the scarf at Ken's neck. "Why do you have this? Where were you when this happened – where IS she?"

Ken began to be frightened. "No, it's not… She lost it yesterday and asked me to help her find it. When she stepped off the path to get it… Honestly, I didn't take it. She was just outside the ruined house, in the underbrush."

"How long ago? Curse it, that must have been what we felt. She's been there hours, we have to hurry." The Green King seemed calmer now. "You've done the right thing, my boy," he. "This is not your fault. Besides which, there's much I have to tell you."

"We don't have time!"

"Oh, someone has already gone for help now, thanks to you. I need you to do something for me now," said the Green King, leading Ken back out of the clearing, back up the hill and over to the ruins.

Ken was inside the ruined house looking out, and what he could see scared him. He didn't know where the Green King had gone or why he had been left in the hut. First, he could see the real woods, damp from the morning dew, quite still. Then they flickered out, as if someone was changing channels on a TV set, and he could see the bright woods, sweet smelling, quiet as the tomb. Then they too flickered out, and the dark woods came into view.

Firstly the dark woods were quiet, and he thought he could see Charlotte, suspended in the thorns, looking very sick and as though she was asleep. He tried jumping out of the hut, but it was as if there was glass across the door. He watched and waited. After an age he saw James arrive and he saw her wake up. The flickering of the woods had slowed, and he

121

had a minute in each one before the scene changed. He saw her crawl through the bushes, and then she and James were gone. An age passed, and as he relaxed, the flickering of the woods began to slow down.

In the bright woods the Green King was walking to the cottage. He hailed Ken just as he flickered out.

The normal world then flicked into view. It was a lovely day, and the sun was getting high in the sky. He saw a squirrel climbing down a tree, and then suddenly he was in the dark woods, and they were alive with the grey creatures.

They were patrolling the paths, all headed in the same direction. He jumped, terrified, and the flickering began to speed up. In the bright woods, the Green King was right outside the hut. "You cannot leave the Watch house, and no one can..." the Green King began before he was cut off.

Sooner than Ken could say anything the dark woods blinked in and he found himself looking right into the eyes of one of the monsters. He jumped, it jumped right at him and everything faded out again. It had seen him. Could it get in? The worlds flicked around, faster and faster.

In the dark woods the thing that had jumped was on the ground, knocked out. Obviously the Green King had been about to tell Ken that no one could get into the house, either. The real woods appeared, and then the Green King flickered back into view.

"Can you see Charlotte? We could sense she was there, but now we can't sense anything..."

"No, she's gone!" he shouted as the woods flickered out.

"Gone or dead, Ken, GONE OR DEAD?" the Green King cried urgently at him and then disappeared again.

Ken sat for a moment, and when the Green King flashed back again he yelled "GONE!!"

"She's alive, then, but we can't find her!" the Green King called back.

Ken stood back at the door and peered out at the changing vistas. In the dark world there was a crowd of the grey things outside the hut, trying to get in. In the bright world, there was the Green King, and now a crowd of green people, also.

In the real world, the house was now ringed by deer, waiting for instructions.

Ken was amazed and confused. What was going on? He asked the Green King, who replied in bits and pieces.

"This place is a neutral outpost between the worlds... You, like your Great-grandfather before you, have been chosen... to be the Watcher, if you so desire. Tonight you have no choice... when things go wrong in the woods you will find yourself coming to this hut... you will be drawn here if the balance is changed in either... either direction. You are the window between the worlds... if you concentrate you can see everything that is happening in all of the woods... lie down and concentrate, tell us what you see..."

Ken did as he was told, and lay down where he had been before, with his head pillowed by a rock. It was comfortable there, very peaceful. He looked up at the trees above the house, changing every few seconds, bright, dark, normal, bright, dark, normal.

He concentrated very hard on the dark woods. The flickering above his head slowed down, and stopped on the bare branches of the trees. A weak, sickly light oozed out of the sky. 'That was easy,' he thought. He turned his head and glanced at the door, then looked away quickly. There were six or seven or the things pressed against the doorway, noses flattened, watching him. He closed his eyes and thought about Charlotte.

A picture began to form in front of his eyes. A dark picture, lit by beams of light, torchlight. Two beams, and the second beam was... James. He realized the Green King must have something to do with James' presence. The caves. They were in the caves. Instantly, he sensed something terrifying. Something more horrifying than anything out in those dark woods already. Something huge and powerful, not quite formed, but almost. Something that was in the caverns with James and Charlotte, something that knew they were there.

He concentrated this time on the bright woods, what he had seen of them. Slowly the trees above him became brighter, greener, the light was warm and healthy. The Green King was still standing by the door.

Ken felt calmer than he ever had before. He seemed to know instinctively what to do.

"They're in the caves, and there's something else in there too, and it's... it's bad," he said. "It's sort of formless or something... but it's getting stronger. I think it's getting ready to move."

The Green King closed his eyes. 'We may be too late,' he thought. "Where is it?"

"It's in the centre, a main cavern or something," Ken replied, trying to remember every detail and wishing he had taken the time to explore the caves.

The Green King shouted something to one of his people, and a group of them peeled off and dashed through the undergrowth, faster than anyone would be able to follow, if anyone had been watching. He turned back to Ken. "You should be able to get a message to them if you think very hard."

Once again, Ken went back to the dark world, concentrated on James and Charlotte, and found them easily. They had reached a fork in the paths, and were uncertain which way to go. If they went forward, it would be about another ten minutes before they hit the main cavern, where all the fear, hatred, pestilence and nameless other dreads were gathering into a ball, and the ball was forming itself into something else...

In the caves, they could hear the noise, and were having a low discussion.

"I think we should go forward," (this was James) "the cavern's the easiest place to cross back. We can get back home before anyone could grab us even if there IS anything there. These chambers echo quite a bit, it may be somewhere else... and you can't walk much farther."

"Nonsense!" insisted Charlotte emphatically. "I can walk. You say that if we take this fork, it'll be about twenty minutes further to exit by the bridge. I'm not going into that cavern. The Green King told me to get out of the woods, and I'm getting out."

Ken could hear them quite plainly. He sent a message. "Go to the bridge... go to the bridge..."

Nothing. He tried harder, squeezing his eyes closed with the effort. He felt as though something had happened. He listened, and with his mind's ear he could hear Charlotte stop speaking.

"Did you hear a voice?" she whispered to James.

"I heard something..."

They stopped so that they could hear better.

Ken tried again, this time relaxing a little. "The bridge... It's Ken!" he added, just in case. This time it definitely got through.

"I hear you!" answered Charlotte. They had both heard him. They looked at each other in the reflected light.

"There's something in the cavern, DON'T GO THERE!"

"Right then," said James, dragging Charlotte through the fork, "I'm with you." Charlotte smiled to herself and thought 'thank you,' back to Ken, even though she knew he wouldn't hear. They started on the long climb back to the surface, no longer capable of wondering how Ken was speaking to them, or how he had found them.

Mrs. Enright and Mrs. Stone were amused, puzzled and angry at their errant children. Yet Mrs. Stone was inclined to let it go, as she was used to Ken taking off at all hours.

"They're just off on a lark," she had told Mrs. Enright over the phone. "Tell you what. I'll leave a note for Ken with his breakfast in case he gets back after Sara's gone to school. I'll just get her ready and if they're not back then, I'll come over around eight thirty. They'll probably go to your house first unless they're close by, Ken knows Charlotte'll be in more trouble... don't worry."

Mrs. Enright sighed and put down the phone. This was most unlike Charlotte. She took the dog everywhere, and Roger was acting very strangely. He refused to come out from under the tree, and had begun to whine slowly under his breath. She had given him his morning bowl of food, but he hadn't touched it. She put out cereal and juice for Charlotte, and put bread in the toaster but didn't press the lever. She then went out to open up the hens for the morning.

They spilled out around her feet in some sort of panic, ignored their feed completely, and went running for the shade of the nearest tree, feathers ruffled, clucking madly to themselves. Very strange. No one wanted breakfast this morning.

She sat down in a lawn chair and waited, nervous for some reason. There were no birds around, and although it was yet another sunny morning with only a few clouds, the entire world seemed silent. She could see the tops of the trees in the woods from her chair, they too were still and quiet. She took a deep breath, beginning to feel afraid.

When Mrs. Stone got to the house, she found Charlotte's mother under the chestnut tree with Roger, leaning against the bark and patting the dog's head.

"Mine too," she said, crouching down and reaching out a hand to Roger's head. He wagged his tail limply, as if he didn't mean it, and lay down, head on his paws, with a big sigh. "All the cats are up trees, and all my dogs are underneath," added Mrs. Stone. "Very peculiar. Must be a storm coming or something. Now come out, let's have some tea."

Charlotte and James were stumbling through the caves. They could hear the sounds becoming more and more distinct, moans becoming growls, getting stronger and stronger, as if something was growing a voice box. They hurried on, Charlotte limping more and more. James had offered to carry her, but the ceiling was too low, it would be impossible. James was counting cross tunnels.

"...Two... alright. We're going to pass a big pillar of rock soon, and we have to go right the first tunnel after that."

They lurched forward again, and came to a pile of rubble.

"I don't remember this," said James. "But the roof falls in once in a while... Don't worry," he added as he heard

126

Charlotte draw in her breath. The two of them continued down the tunnel. A few metres past the rock fall, Charlotte stepped on a fallen rock, stumbled and fell on her ankle.

"OW!" she hissed between clenched teeth. James came over and helped her up. She was alright, but she'd skinned her knee slightly. She barely even felt it through the stinging of the cuts made by the thorns. She felt awful, but in the light of his torch he could see that she was looking better, her skin was pinker, her eyes didn't look as sunken. Her whole body ached, though, and her foot was so swollen that her shoe cut into it. She had a headache, and she'd already drank half the water because she was so thirsty. "It's cold in here," she complained. James flashed his light at her.

"No wonder you feel so cold, you're barely wearing anything. Here. Take my jacket." He yanked off his jacket, and she put it on. It was warm, and on her it went almost to her knees. She thanked him, and they hurried on down the tunnel.

They had made another try to get back to their own world, quickly while Charlotte took a rest and put on the jacket, but James couldn't even cross back by himself. Something was definitely stopping them. They didn't try it again for fear of attracting unwanted attention.

"You know when you've crossed back, down here," James had said earlier "There's lots of water running down the walls on the home side, quite a few puddles, and it smells earthy, the air's fresher on our side."

They walked for five minutes more, and then James cursed to himself. "Damn fool, Charlotte you're not going to like this, but we've got to go back to the rock-fall.

"What? Why?" He was right. She didn't like that. It was five minutes back, so they would have wasted ten minutes, and the noises behind them weren't letting up at all. In fact, they were getting much louder, and she didn't know how much time they actually had.

"That rock fall must have been the pillar, you probably fell right when we reached the tunnel mouth, and I was too stupid to notice. We walked past it already, I recognise this

127

tunnel because it's so square..." he motioned to the mouth of a tunnel behind him with his light. It was very regular, square cut, almost. "It's the one after the tunnel we want. We've got to go back."

Charlotte's mouth was dry, and not from thirst. She was listening to the sounds behind them, and she had heard movement. Her throat was tense, it felt as if her heart was sitting in it, making a big lump that stopped her from breathing, talking, moving. She shook her head wildly at James.

"What's wrong... Charlotte!" He stepped towards her, and then he heard the noise too.

Something moving along the tunnel behind them, scraping the walls, dragging rocks along with it... getting closer. Did they have enough time? They didn't have time to find out. He grabbed her hand, and they ran down the square tunnel as fast as they could.

"Where does this go?" asked Charlotte, panting. She wanted to fall down and stay down, but fear was keeping her on her feet.

"It goes straight for a while and then branches," answered James. "One branch goes back to the cavern, the other peters out after a while, I've never really gone down that way much, I think it's a dead end."

'Great!' thought Charlotte. The last thing they needed was a path to the main cavern. Whatever had been in there would be able to get back easily enough. And who was to say there wasn't two of whatever it was? More even? They ran for a while, Charlotte hobbling more than running.

In the Watcher's house, Ken was trying to find James and Charlotte. They weren't in the same tunnel anymore, and he cast around looking for them, and came across... Blinding visions of darkness sucked him away. He felt his mind fall into a maelstrom of fear, hatred. Somehow he could feel a burning, scraping sensation. He felt a terrible feeling, like he was being sucked out of his body like a snail from its shell – this thing was more powerful, more horrible than anything he'd ever thought could exist. He beat his fist on the ground beside him, harder and harder, trying to will himself to wake up.

His mind was slowly being wrenched from his body. He fought as hard as he could, and just when he thought he was gone for good, whatever it was let go a little and he felt himself return to his body. The fabric of his T-shirt was protecting more than his body. He wrapped Charlotte's scarf tighter around him.

He flipped to the Bright woods and called out to the Green King: "It's alive, it's walking around!" and then right away flipped back to the Dark world. It was easy, as if he'd been doing it for his whole life.

He let loose the scarf and felt along the caves again, this time avoiding where he knew the thing to be. His searching mind found Charlotte and James rushing along a new tunnel, a dead end. In panic, he felt along the length of the cave, looking for a way out.

This tunnel was different, Ken realized. It was man-made, really man-made. There was another tunnel that joined it, but the entrance was obscured, covered over by blocks of stone. A doorway! A doorway only a few yards ahead of the two fleeing figures. He concentrated, and made contact easily.

"James, Charlotte!" They heard him and slowed down.

His entry into the mind of the Black being had stopped it for a moment, given them a fraction more time. Hearing the silence, they stopped. "You're approaching a hidden door, just ahead. Keep going..." they walked a few paces, slowly as Ken directed them. When he said 'stop', they stopped. Behind them the noise was beginning again. They only had a few moments.

Ken felt around with his mind. There was a ring recessed into one of the blocks and covered with a flake of stone, thin as card, riveted to the door at its top edge. Perfectly camouflaged.

"See the blocks?" came Ken's voice in their minds.

James shone his torch on the wall, found them and gaped in surprise. He'd never seen the blocks before, never been down this far or looked at the wall with his torch before.

129

"Four blocks up, that small one, it's fake, swing it aside, try turning the ring underneath. And HURRY!!" Ken's voice rang in their minds. Charlotte saw it, reached in front of James and swivelled the flake up, revealing the ring. James turned the ring and the blocks creaked back. They too were fake, only a few inches thick. The door was only wood underneath, and the hinges were perfectly balanced. They tumbled through the entrance and between them, rammed the door shut. The slamming of the door made the flake of stone fall back down over the ring, and once again there was nothing to be seen. They shone their lights into the passageway in front of them. It, too, was carved out of the bedrock. There were ancient metal fittings on the walls for candles, and dust lay thickly everywhere. The air was stale but breathable, as there were small vents drilled into the ceiling.

Slowly, spiderwebs began to appear. With the thing in the corridors now safely on the other side of the door, and this new tunnel in front of them, James and Charlotte were making the transition back to their own world easily.

In the Watcher's hut, Ken reported them safe to a much relieved Green King.

"It's time for you and I to have a talk," he said. Ken nodded through the door, mutely. He was unbelievably curious. So many new things had happened, so many questions were running through his mind. He felt the air in front of his face, but he still could not pass through the door.

"You cannot cross," said the Green King, sadly. "Now, you are the Watcher. If you choose to be the Watcher for always, you will be able to see everything in all the lands, but you will not be able to cross outside of your own. You will not be part of my world, and you will not be part of the dark world. Both will be closed to you, forever."

Ken felt a slow ache inside him for the things he'd never see with his own eyes, never touch with his hands, air he would never breathe. He'd just discovered new worlds but

130

would forever be a Watcher.

He stopped himself. He'd just been given powers beyond anything anyone he knew possessed, powers to see anything, anywhere. While he was in the hut, he knew that even outside the woods he would know what was happening, and while the doors was closed, even in his own world he could see things, everything in the woods, and around them. If he took the job. There was no doubt in his mind. Of course he would take the job. And, what was it the Green King had said about his Great-Grandfather?

He looked at the Green King. "Can I refuse?" he asked, even though he already knew that he would do it.

The Green King smiled sadly. "Yes, you can. Nothing is final, although I doubt you'll refuse. You've been hand-picked, you see," he stopped. "Still, all this belongs to another time. Right now, you must return home. You must go to Charlotte's mother and beg forgiveness, tell her that the two of you went for an early walk and expected to be home. You went farther than you thought and lost track of time. Since she was so close to Rosemary's house on the other side of the woods she is there for breakfast, and is borrowing a uniform. Tell her that Rosemary's telephone is out and that Charlotte will ring during the first break. You are to contact Charlotte and tell her the same. Then you are to go home and to school as normal. When you see Rosemary, give her the same message.

"I know Rosemary," he said in response to Ken's questioning look, "she will do as you ask. No more questions, I will see you sooner than you want. Things are afoot, gather your strength!" and with that Ken found himself looking into the eyes of the grey stag, which then bounded out of sight, leaving the bright woods empty and silent.

He lay back down, mind whirling, and prepared to contact Charlotte one last time.

In the tunnel, James and Charlotte were walking for what

seemed like ages. Charlotte listened to Ken, and before she could ask him for directions out, he was gone.

"Well thanks a LOT!" she yelled to the thin air and collapsed onto the floor, legs in front of her. She massaged her ankle.

"Come on," said James. "How's your foot?"

"I can't go much further," she cried. "I think I'm going to have to cut my shoe off."

James crouched beside her. He shone his light on the shoe. Charlotte's leg where it emerged from her running shoe was violently discoloured. There were several scratches and one deep cut, each one a nasty mixture of yellow and black, with blood still seeping slowly from each one. The rest of her skin was bruised blue and purple, and the top of the shoe was buried in swollen flesh. Very nasty indeed, he wondered if she'd actually broken the bone.

He reached into his boot and drew out a hunting knife, identical to the one that Ken carried.

Charlotte reached for it. "Ken's got one just like this," she observed.

"Really?" asked James, very surprised. "I found this in the woods a long time ago... the black woods. Hold very still now, I'm taking your shoe off."

Charlotte winced at the idea. She drew in her breath and held it.

James looked at her. She let it out. "All I'm going to do is untie the laces first. You want to do it instead?"

She nodded. She untied the laces, and the pressure eased quite a bit. She unthreaded them completely, but the shoe was still cutting into her foot. She tried to ease it off, but it wouldn't come.

"Now, do you want to keep it on like that, or shall I cut it?" asked James. Charlotte thought for a bit. It did feel better without the laces. She decided that a painful shoe was better than no shoe. She stood up.

"Guess you made up your mind then," grinned James. "Atta girl! Just don't put any weight on it, take my arm."

He put his knife back in his boot, straightened up, reached

around and picked her up like a baby – the ceiling was far too low for piggybacking.

Together they continued down the tunnel, avoiding the odd spiderweb ("Wonder what they find to eat in here?" James pondered). Another ten minutes passed, and they reached a dead end with two wooden doors, identical to the inside of the one they had come through earlier. One at the very end, and the other a few feet away on the right hand wall. Each one had a matching ring handle to the one on the other door.

"Which door, you reckon?" asked James. "The one straight ahead or the one to the right?"

Charlotte shrugged. "Let's try the one at the end, first."

They turned the ring, heaved on the door, and like the first, it swung slowly open. A pile of boxes crashed to the floor. James jumped, nearly dropping Charlotte and hitting his head in the process.

"OW! Damn!" He rubbed his head as they shone their lights on the pile. Cardboard. Modern, or at least made in the last thirty years. They had labels on them, numbered.

Charlotte was the first to notice that there was a pale light seeping in from somewhere. "I think we're in a building somewhere. A cellar."

"Definitely. Wonder whose it is?" They climbed over the boxes, and looked around the room. It was filled with similar boxes, some on shelves, others just piled against the wall. The boxes that had been leaning on the door had been stacked rather haphazardly, and were covered in dust. They restacked them, leaving a small path in the middle leading to the doorway. Charlotte left her torch behind, for when they returned later, as she thought they probably would.

The doorway had been wallpapered over years ago. Where it had opened, the wallpaper hung in tatters. Fortunately the wallpaper and paint around most of the room was in a similar condition. ('Wonder if there's any more tunnels?' thought Charlotte). James ran his hand over the wall until he felt the raised stone where he knew the ring would be and slit the paper. It peeled away easily, and he cut it into a neat flap, exposing the slate. He tugged at the stone until it swung around to reveal the ring, tested it a few times, then replaced the slate and the paper. "That way," he said, "We can get back out if we 'ave to". Privately, Charlotte wondered why on earth they'd want to go back.

They walked to where a slice of yellow light was showing through a crack, and found the way out. The door opened into a stairwell with a light at the top. They crept up the stairs and listened through the door.

They heard: "If you look on the wall to your right, you'll see a portrait of the very first Porter in this town, James Alfred Porter... Next, his son, Edward Porter the first..." and then after a moment they heard the sound of several feet walking on wood floors.

They were in the museum, the old Porter manor, and the museum guide was leading around a new trainee before the museum opened.

James opened the door a crack, looked out, and then gave Charlotte the thumbs up. They crept out, and snuck around a corner. James knew his way around, and guided them successfully through to a side door, and out into the daylight.

It was almost ten o'clock, Charlotte realized, too late to go to Rosemary's and borrow clothes. She was skiving out on the last day of school - and so was James, she realized.

"Do you have any money I can borrow?" she asked James, "I've got to use a telephone."

"Use my mobile," said James, digging into his pocket. Charlotte dialled her house.

"Um...hi Mum, it's Charlotte..."

"Charlotte, where on EARTH have you been?" her mother's voice came down the line, tight with worry and anger. "I've been worried sick about you all morning. If Ken hadn't come by exactly when he did, I'd have phoned the police..." she stopped. "Anyway," she continued in a better frame of mind, "is everything alright?"

"Fine Mum," lied Charlotte.

"Are you at school?"

"Yes. I'm so sorry, I won't do it again. I was just walking, I forgot the time..."

"Alright, but you are NEVER to do this again. Furthermore, if you want to go anywhere again, you have to check with me first. You are grounded for... for... for ages." Her mother sounded mollified but still cross, and Charlotte breathed a small sigh of relief. Step one completed. Now she just had to do something about her clothes and her ankle.

"I have to get back to class now," she said, thinking fast.

"I'll see you when you get home," her mother replied, still angry.

"OK. Sorry, Mum... love you."

"Love you too, Charlotte. See you later," said Mrs. Enright as she hung up the telephone.

Charlotte was tired. She hadn't slept in 24 hours, hadn't eaten, had only a few sips of water. She'd been drugged, scratched, chased, and she had a bad injury to her ankle. Now she couldn't go to school, and she couldn't go home without having to explain everything.

James was still sitting by the telephone booth, looking at her worriedly. He wasn't used to worrying about other people, normally he didn't much care; but she'd seen the dark woods now, she knew his secret, he supposed he'd better look after her.

"You can't go around like that, you know. There's already been some busybody giving you the once over. Hope it was no one you know. We've got to get you out of whatever it is you're wearing, and into some bandages for that foot."

Charlotte climbed onto the bench beside him and slumped against James with the jacket she'd borrowed from him pulled down as far as it would go over her knees, leaning slightly against the older boy, eyes half closed. James thought for a bit, and his brow cleared.

"I've got a mate a few streets away, you might even know him, Simon Brook. Actually, you'd probably know his brother, Tony. He'd be in your year, maybe the next..."

"I know him," interrupted Charlotte. "Rosemary's going out with him or something."

"Alright then," smiled James in his soft county burr. "Well, his older brother Simon went to school with Ted, and I've

135

known him for years. He'd probably be home, probably still in bed, the lazy sod, and he'll give us a hand. He lives so close, can you walk a little?" he asked, standing up and brushing himself off.

Charlotte smiled, wryly. She'd gotten this far, she could certainly walk to safety. She stood, and waves of pain and nausea swirled around her stomach. She bent forward, putting painful pressure on her foot, and closed her eyes until it went away. "I'm alright," she gasped, "just dizzy."

"'Just dizzy' my foot!" said James. He reached over and to her surprise he hoisted her up so that she was standing on one leg on the bench. "Turn around and face me," he ordered, and then presented his back to her. "I'm going to piggyback you to Simon's house."

Charlotte grabbed James around the neck, and for the third time that morning was carried by James. He lifted her up, and they set off towards Simon's house, catching the occasional stare from morning passers-by, young women with prams, old men out for their morning constitutional and the like.

They arrived, after a few minutes, at a pink bungalow in a row of identical bungalows, all painted various bright, and clashing, colours.

Simon was, indeed, still in bed. James set Charlotte down on the lawn in front of the cheery little bungalow, and banged on the door. After there was no answer the third time in a row, James told Charlotte he'd be right back, and he scooted around to the back of the house, where she could hear him yelling various unsavoury things, presumably at a window. Presently she heard the beeping of James' mobile phone buttons, and inside the house the phone started to ring. And ring and ring and ring.

She curled up on the damp grass, not caring about the dew at this point. She could see the world through the stems of grass, tinted green. Simon's house had a small patch of lawn at the front, and a low fence with an iron gate in it ran from one side to the other. There were a few flowering plants in borders, but the lawn needed mowing and the borders needed weeding. She was just beginning to doze off when James came back around to the front of the house and shook her.

"Simon's getting out of bed and coming around to let us in."

Charlotte opened her eyes sleepily. "Won't his parents mind?"

"No" said James, with a chuckle. "Simon lives on his own here... He makes a killing doing shift management over at the mill."

"He owns his own house?" Charlotte managed to be amazed through her exhaustion.

"Naw, just rents it, used to be his grandmother's and he gets it cheap from his Mum and Dad."

They were interrupted by the door opening, and a very dishevelled looking Simon sagged out, grimacing and blocking the sun from his eyes.

"What you doing here this time in the morning? I only got to sleep at three... This better be worth it... Come on, get inside, it's too bright..." he staggered, still half awake, into the depths of the little house, and James and Charlotte tottered in after him.

Chapter 11

"Hallo Charlotte, what on earth have you been up to then?" Simon was standing in his living room giving Charlotte and James a good look.

"And you," he directed at James without waiting for an answer, "you look like you've been through hell. Give me a moment will you, I'm going to put some real clothes on..." and he staggered off down the hall knuckling his eyes, disappeared into a room, then reappeared briefly "Go put some tea on or something, will you?" and with that there was silence.

James smiled and shook his head. He waved Charlotte into the kitchen, and sat her down at the scruffy table. It was a gloomy kitchen, full of dishes both washed and unwashed, a pot of something burned and dried out on the stove, a few pieces of clothing on the floor, and several mugs half full of cold tea sitting on the table, along with old bills, coins, yesterday's paper, and piles of other junk that seemed to have been forgotten about.

"Ugh!" shuddered Charlotte, involuntarily.

"I know. Not much to look at, is it?" laughed James. "I imagine he only cleans it up when his Mum comes around. Wonder what his girl thinks about it?" he chuckled some more at that thought, and puddled around cleaning mugs and locating the tea.

There was a mirror on the wall, and Charlotte got up and examined herself in the mirror. No wonder people had stared, it wasn't only her clothes that were filthy and in shreds. Her face had a couple of small scratches on it, and it was filthy - a combination of the dusty caves and crawling on the ground back in... The realization of what had actually happened that night stopped her.

"Did we really, I mean, was that all... you know...?" she asked, slowly.

"Real? Course. Mind you, you've never been there before, have you?" James rinsed out the teapot and put in new bags. He located the kettle, peered dubiously inside, filled it with

138

water and plugged it in. He sat down at the table. Charlotte noticed he was shivering a little. She felt cold herself. She sat down at the table.

"No," she answered him, finally. "I've never been there before. I've only been to the other woods."

James looked at her and then looked down at his feet. His voice was quiet all of a sudden. "I was there once," he muttered, and then said nothing more.

Charlotte looked at the older boy. His hair was filthy, he looked as bad as she, and he was obviously as unnerved as she – plus he'd spent a large part of the last few hours carrying her about.

She was suddenly too tired to do anything. Her foot had stopped throbbing quite as badly as it had been, but her shoe had to come off soon. The kettle boiled and Simon returned fully dressed from the bedroom at the same time. James pasted a smile onto his face and got up to finish making the tea.

Charlotte's head was getting heavier and heavier. She cleared a clean spot in front of her with her elbows, and pillowed her head in her arms on the table.

When she woke up, she was lying on Simon's ratty brown couch, covered with a blanket. Her head was clearer, and the sun was higher in the sky. She could hear the definite sounds of dishes being washed in the other room, and the low voices of the boys, chatting back and forth.

She closed her eyes, but she couldn't get back to sleep. She kept worrying in her mind about everything. About the time - she had to be home on real school hours, about her foot, about the woods, about Ken... But mostly about the thing roaming in the caves under the dark woods. And she was starving.

She realized it was no good, she'd never get back to sleep. She sat up, and swung her legs in front of her. Her shoes were gone, both of them. She must have been out of it, she thought, for the boys to have gotten her running shoe off her swollen ankle without her waking up screaming in pain.

She stretched her legs out in front of her and examined

139

herself. Her ankle was really puffy, and a bright purple-blue colour from her toes all the way to her knee. It was throbbing, but not too badly but the cuts were nasty looking. She was going to have some explaining to do when she got home...

She lurched onto her good foot, and with the blanket still wrapped around her she limped into the kitchen.

The boys had cleaned up quite well, and she supposed James had shamed Simon into it. She wondered what James had actually told the other boy. As she walked in, they turned around and smiled at her.

"What time is it?" she croaked.

"Only twelve thirty, you can sleep some more if you like," James replied, seemingly oblivious to the fact that he hadn't slept all night either. He looked clean and refreshed, his hair was still damp from the bath he must have just had.

"I can't, I keep thinking about everything I have to do."

"Like what?" asked Simon.

"Like, clean up, find some clothes, figure out what to tell my mother, get home on time..." she said, indignantly, looking at James questioningly.

"It's alright," said James. "I told Simon what happened." He grimaced at her meaningfully behind Simon's back.

"You did?" she asked, dumbfounded.

"Yeah," said Simon. "You gotta be careful in those caves, lucky for you James came along when he did looking for those bats he's always on about that live down there. You might have gotten lost." He looked at her, reprovingly, but not without humour.

James cleared his throat as she turned to look at him with her eyebrows raised. "Yes," she said, looking right at James. "Lucky for me," she added sarcastically, "oh yeah, strong boy rescues foolish girl from the caves..." And then she remembered that James had indeed rescued her, although not quite the way he'd put it. It would make a good story, anyway. She wondered if James had mentioned the secret passageway they'd found.

"Do you have an extra towel?" she asked, changing the

subject.

"Yeah. Wanna borrow some clothes?" asked Simon. James looked at him, surprised.

"Well, she can't go about with her own clothes. I've got a few old T-shirts, and I'm sure Tony's left some clothes here for when he stays over, she'd fit into his jeans, maybe with a belt," he added, looking at Charlotte's thin wrists.

They ran her a bath (Charlotte made certain that the tub was clean) and afterwards, feeling fresh and dressed, with her wounds smarting a little from disinfectant, Charlotte felt much better. As part of his training for work, Simon knew a lot of first aid and had a good kit at his house, unlikely as it seemed that he could have anything that useful in the tip he lived in.

Her shoes were alright, although she could only wear one. Simon lent her a pair of thick socks and she put them both on her swollen foot, as a kind of slipper.

"I'm going to drive over to the school and pick up Tony and Rosemary," said Simon "then maybe you can borrow some of her clothes before you go home. You go with James, show the teachers your foot and make up some story. They'll understand, besides it is the last day of school. You can get your report card and James can get his, and your mother will never know the difference. We'll ride you home, too."

"Thank you so much," breathed Charlotte, a little overwhelmed at the help she was getting. "If there's every anything I can do for you, I owe you one..."

Simon laughed. "Alright," he said, "what ever... Now, food."

By the time three o'clock rolled around, they'd eaten eggs, toast, baked beans and a toasted cheese sandwich because Charlotte was still hungry. She, unable to stand the mess in the place had also shamed Simon into cleaning up even more, with her sitting in the living room directing - "What about that pile of CDs?..." - every time Simon claimed he was finished. Charlotte and James were getting a little hysterical and giggly from their lack of sleep. They kept finding new things to do until Simon finally gave them one last filthy look and collapsed on a couch.

"Susan's never going to believe this," said Simon, surveying the damage. "I don't think the place has ever been this clean. Maybe she'll visit more often now..." he added ruefully, as James snorted his tea through his nose laughing. "And as for you two," he said, gazing at James and Charlotte, now hysterical with laughter, "next time you come over, either of you, I want fair warning."

The two adventurers nodded and smirked silently, each wiping tears from their eyes.

At the school, Charlotte limped into her last class, and presented her foot to the teacher, claiming she'd had to stay home, but came to get her report card. The teacher wasn't upset at all; Ken had claimed he was passing the message from Charlotte's Mum that she wasn't coming in, and after looking at Charlotte's foot she wondered aloud why she'd even bothered. "We could have posted your report card you know," she said.

The students were milling around, picking up final assignments and making last minute plans for the summer. Rosemary was easy to track down, she was in the hallway outside the classroom chatting with Ken and Tony. They greeted Charlotte with wide eyes, and she told them the story that James had told Simon, with a sidelong glance at Ken. Ken hadn't told Rosemary anything other than the fake message for Charlotte's mother, just in case. When the bell rang, they headed out to the waiting car and drove over to Rosemary's house.

Rosemary did indeed live close to the outskirts of the woods, in fact, quite close to the museum as well as close to Simon, and Tony. It was a small suburban area, quite close to the factories and the mills. Tony's house was the furthest away, and the house Simon lived in was on the same street as Rosemary.

Charlotte and Rosemary weren't the same size, but nonetheless Charlotte fit into yet another borrowed shirt and pair of old jeans, and they set off to her house.

Most of Charlotte's own clothes were ruined beyond

repair. Her pyjama shirt was salvageable but the rest of her clothes, shirt, jeans and pyjama bottoms were not even useful as rags. Luckily they were her oldest clothes...

Charlotte bought herself up with a start. It seemed to her as though ages had passed, not merely a day and a night. She'd only gotten about two hours of sleep at Simon's house and it wasn't enough, she was getting extremely tired. She glanced at James and Ken. Both of them looked exhausted. Neither one of them had gotten even two hours of sleep. She hoped they wouldn't be called on that night, as none of them would be any use at all to the Green King.

They drove her home in silence, leaving Rosemary and Tony behind at Rosemary's house.

"You're a cheery lot!" chirped Simon, into the emptiness.

"I didn't get any sleep last night," said Ken, "sorry".

"What is this? The stay-up-all-night-club? What were you doing, out in the caves too?" asked Simon, looking over at Ken, slumped in the passenger seat. He looked in the rear view mirror. James and Charlotte were each leaning against their own side of the car, eyes closed.

Ken looked at Simon and snorted. "Naw... can't stand caves. Too claustrophobic for me, I keep feeling the roof's going to fall in."

"Yeah, me too. You heard about her, then?" said Simon with a jerk of his head to the back seat where Charlotte was apparently asleep, "got lost in the caves..."

"I didn't get lost," murmured Charlotte, as righteously as she could muster through her drowsy sleep. "I just sprained my ankle. But don't tell my Mom, she's got to think that I did this just now... never let me outside again..." she petered out.

"Well this is a cheery drive," Simon remarked to the silence.

Charlotte told her parents that she'd been showing off at the hurdles after school and missed one which had scratched her on the way down. She half dozed all through supper, and went straight to bed afterwards. Her Mother came in with an ice pack for her ankle, but Charlotte was asleep before she

143

had finished propping up the leg. She sat by her daughter watching her sleep for a while with a worried look on her face.

Ken's mother looked him up and down, recognised instantly that he was exhausted, and sat him down with something to eat quickly. Neither his sister or his father noticed anything, for which he was intensely glad. After he'd eaten, he was so tired that he crept up to bed without saying goodnight to anyone, and after putting Charlotte's scarf under his mattress, he crawled into bed and was asleep before he'd even turned off the light. Later, his mother turned it off for him, creeping out quietly and closing the door behind her. She had an idea what might be happening.

At James' house, it was a different matter. He was in a lot of trouble with his father for not doing his morning chores on the farm, and had to go out after supper and do extra duty in the sheep sheds.

Eventually his father came to get him. "Alright, off home with the lot of you," said old Ted. He looked at James in the light from the barn. "You need to get yourself cleaned up. Come on."

The two walked in silence back to the house, the dogs trotting along behind. "You worried your Ma half mad this morning. She went into the woods and spent a couple of hours looking for you. She called the school and you weren't there, she'd have called half the town if I hadn't have stopped her. You could have telephoned, you know."

"I figured you'd all think I was in school. I'm sorry, I went for a walk this morning and lost track of time. I'll catch up on things tomorrow. I spent the day at Simon's house," he added, truthfully "helping him clean up. It's a pig-sty over there..."

"You're not so clean yourself. Should've known you'd be with Simon. Now don't go doing this again or I swear I won't let you off the farm the rest of the summer. You don't half need a bath too," said his father, looking him up and down in the shadow. James knew his father couldn't really see him, but he could certainly smell him. The brief clean-up

144

James had given himself at Simon's had long worn off, he stank of sheep and sweat.

James shrugged. His Dad wasn't so bad, just a little cross. It was almost impossible to get him angry, but shirking chores was guaranteed to get him steaming. They trudged on, the lights from the house and the yard giving a pleasant glow to the night. Each blade of grass threw a tall, spiky shadow of its own down the hill. There was a wind coming up, and the weather forecast for the next day predicted that the long sunny period was ending.

'Typical,' thought James to himself as they reached the yard. 'Bad weather on the first day out of school.' The wind was chill, colder than usual for the time of year. James snorted to himself. Once home, he had peeled off most of his clothes on the way up the stairs to his room. There, he got out of everything, bundled it all up and threw it in the laundry bin, and had two baths, one which lasted about ten minutes after which the tub looked more like it was filled with water from the cow's trough than anything, and another long one in cleaner water. He soaked until he was completely clean, until his skin was crumpled and pink and then longer until the water was cold and his brother hammered on the door that it was late, and that he wanted his turn. James had no recollection the next day of getting out of the bath and into bed.

The night was cooling down fast. Clouds were drifting gently across the face of the moon, birds were huddled against tree trunks puffed out like feather dusters. Out in the Starling's pasture, all the cows were gathered in one corner high up the hill against the shed, lying down. Number 211 lifted her head briefly and looked up. Whether or not she was considering the weather, no one can know, but she - and the other cows - knew something. They felt a storm coming, and they were nervous. She settled her head back down, and went on chewing her cud and blowing air gently through her nose.

In the clearing, all was not quiet. It teemed with life; there were torches lit under the trees, and the huts off in the darkness glimmered through the foliage. The bright woods were moving. The trees were thrashing around, sending leafy messages, tightening their roots in the soil. In our world, the woods rustled independent of any wind, and ground animals dug themselves deeply into their burrows, or foraged fearfully amongst the brambles and ferns, alert to every unusual sound.

The Green King and his Lady were holding court. Nothing could be heard by human ears, even if anyone had been crouching in the bracken to listen. Not a sound came over the wind, but the Lady was speaking to her people.

"It's time." The people shifted nervously. "We are not powerless." They looked at her, fearfully. She was shining with her own light, dwarfing the Green King beside her, brighter than the moonshine filtering through the trees. "We must be prepared."

In our world, a flock of deer appeared in the clearing out of nowhere, and with much twitching of ears and stomping of feet they bounded off into the centre of the woods. The grey stag at the forefront leapt away so quickly, it seemed as though he disappeared. Soon, there was nothing to be seen, and little to be heard except for the slow hissing of a young wind, gathering strength.

Chapter 12

The next morning was overcast and soggy. Rain fell down in slow blotches, big as marbles, splatting slowly down onto windows. The sky bulged pregnant with black clouds. There was fog everywhere on the ground, the air was warm and far in the distance soft rumblings could be heard. It was right on the brink of beginning the biggest storm that the town had seen for years.

Ken telephoned Charlotte and asked if he could come over after breakfast. When he was halfway across the field separating the two houses, the spots of rain started to come down faster, and by the time he had run all the way across, the storm had hit.

The two of them sat in Charlotte's living room with mugs of hot chocolate. Mrs. Enright got the fireplace going, but not before she'd run outside to protect her young tomato plants. After the fire was roaring, she left Ken and Charlotte with a plate of food and a pack of cards and dashed off into the rain to the shed. She was building some plant frames and wasn't going to let the rain stop her. She whistled for the dog to follow her. Roger stood at the door looking into the rain, stepped out about two steps and then ran back inside. Charlotte closed the door behind him, and hobbled back to her seat in the living room. The dog settled down as close to the fire as he could get and sighed himself to sleep. No more walks for him today.

"How's yer leg?" Ken asked Charlotte into the silence that followed.

"Not too bad," answered Charlotte. "If it's not gone down by the end of the day Mum's going to make go to the hospital for an x-ray. It's already down a bit though," she said, raising her leg off the cushion it was on, "See? It's not half as swollen as before. It's still purple but I think it's ok."

Ken grimaced at the bruised skin on Charlotte's leg. He looked at his hands for a while and then looked up suddenly, smiling. "Hey, I almost forgot!" he said brightly. He reached under his shirt and he pulled out Charlotte's scarf.

"My scarf!" yelled Charlotte, and reached out for it. "Where did you find it?" she grabbed it happily, ran the fabric through her fingers.

"It was right where you saw it, but it just didn't... cross over... with you. I picked it up and forgot to tell you yesterday."

"Wow. Thanks a lot, Ken. I can't believe that all happened yesterday morning. It felt like such a long time... I wonder what's going to happen next...?" She trailed off, there was too much to talk about.

Now the subject of the woods had been bought up, they both fell silent. They started playing cards, not talking except about the game. Soon, all there was to hear in the room was the slow flipping of cards against a background of falling rain. Ken was the first one to speak.

"Well, after yesterday we all know what everything's about, anyway," he began.

"Yeah, I guess so," said Charlotte.

Ken paused, played a card and discarded another. "Now I suppose we have to think of a way to get rid of that *thing*," he said, immediately moving on to more practical matters. "I tell you, it's not going to be easy at all. I saw into its mind for a moment... It almost didn't let me go... Ugh!"

They both shuddered. Charlotte said, "I don't know how big it was, or how big the cave exits are. If it can cross over to our world inside the caves, it may be trapped in there. Of course it may be able to ooze through." She was silent for a second, panic rising in her stomach.

"Ken, what do we do if it gets out?" she wailed. "What happens if it knows who we are and shows up at our houses? What happens if it gets into the town? Is it going to keep growing?" she trailed off, horrified.

Ken seemed pretty calm in comparison. "I got a, well, a look at it, I think. It's pretty bad. It's big, and I think it's blind. It was bumping into the walls all over the place, going by smell or something. I don't think it's finished forming yet. It could turn itself into anything, split into lots of little versions, I don't know. In fact, the chances are good that it'll

148

form itself into something that looks human. That's probably all it knows. Humans and those things in the dark woods."

"I wonder what those were?" asked Charlotte. "Those woods are pretty awful, but originally the only danger there was the fear, you know, the fog. And the thorns. Just like in the bright woods. The only things in the bright woods are the animals, and they can go anywhere they want, I thought. Into any of the worlds."

"Don't forget the green people," interrupted Ken. "They live in the bright woods."

"But they're different. They were originally people that crossed over and wanted to stay... oh." Charlotte and Ken looked at each other. They both had the same thought.

"Hmm," puzzled Ken. "But why would anyone want to stay in the dark woods. Wouldn't the fear make them too frightened to stay? What would they eat? Why wouldn't they cross back?"

Charlotte had a sudden idea. "Remember that tunnel from the museum?"

"Yes," answered Ken, "what about it?"

"Well, why was that built?"

"Probably a getaway for the Porters, remember it used to be their house, the Museum. They might have had an exit they used, some way they could leave the manor unnoticed. They had lots of enemies, you know. People thought they were thieves, too. There were a lot of robberies back then in neighbouring towns but never here. Apparently there was even proof that one of the Porters was involved, but they never did anything about it."

"They're your ancestors, aren't they?" Charlotte was interested in the Porters. Somehow things seemed to lead back to that old, dead family. If Ken was to be believed, there were no living members of that family apart from him and his mother. He was the last. There was also the mystery of Ken's great-grandfather, who had appeared from nowhere, married the last of the Porters and then disappeared.

"Yes, they were." Ken looked up, the fire of interest in his eyes. He'd done a lot of research about his ancestors. That tunnel might answer the last of his questions. "Are we still going to go to the museum?" he asked.

"Sure," said Charlotte, understanding at once. "I could ask Mum if we could go today. She was trying to think of something for this afternoon, I think she was going to call your Mum. Let's see if they want to go! We can leave them behind and you can show me around the museum! I think I can walk alright." She was cheered up quite a bit by the thought. "At least we'll be doing something, instead of sitting here. Maybe we can sneak down and I'll show you the tunnel."

"I want to check out that other door, you know, the one beside the one you came in through. Hmm. I just had a thought." said Ken, his brows moving together slightly, thinking. "Remember I told you about the people who lived in my house before my great-grandfather?"

"Yes," said Charlotte, waiting for him to go on.

"Remember I said that they went missing?"

"Yes," she said slowly, understanding forming in the back of her mind. "Could the Porters have sent them into the caves? Maybe they thought they'd get lost down there. Maybe they had someone waiting in the caves to kill them. Maybe, just maybe mind you, they were running in fear from the killers, and crossed over into the dark woods without knowing it. If they got out into the dark woods they wouldn't have known how to cross back. They would have been trapped in there... Oh. What they have eaten?"

"James said he saw one catch a fox, once. I didn't get hungry while I was there, and James didn't even get that thirsty. Maybe you stop having to eat or drink as much there. I know that James and I started to look grey just from being there a few hours. If you were there even a week you'd probably start to change."

Ken was excited. "That would explain a lot of things. There were quite a few other missing people that were connected to the Porters. Maybe they knew about the dark woods, and put people there on purpose."

"I think I remember the Green King telling me that they only started sensing actual beings in there a few hundred years ago. Maybe that's why the fog has only just started to coalesce into something more solid." A nasty suspicion was forming at the back of Charlotte's mind. Ken shifted uncomfortably in his seat.

"I think I know what you're getting at," he said darkly. "What if something in particular caused it to happen? Something caused by men... Who, though?"

"I don't know. Maybe there really used to be such things as magic. Good magicians and bad ones. I mean, the Green King's not normal. I'd say he was magic, wouldn't you?"

"Naw!" scoffed Ken. "It's not magic, it's just another world... Haven't you read any science fiction?"

"Yes," answered Charlotte. "I already thought of that."

"Science doesn't know everything yet. If you went back four hundred years with a torch they'd burn you as a witch. There's things that exist that science can't explain. I don't think it's magic. Maybe there are lots of undiscovered worlds around, full of undiscovered science. Occasionally someone may stumble on the way through to one of them. Maybe the all the worlds have always existed, but they've only recently become solid, as more and more things cross over into each one, " Ken went on excitedly. "So, since most people would rather be happy than sad, more animals would rather be warm than cold, and plants are naturally peaceful, the good world filled up faster."

"And," Charlotte continued, "now there's so many people in our world, with pollution and war happening on a bigger scale, there's more stuff to fill the dark world." She knitted her brows together. "So, how are we going to stop that thing from getting out? Even if we stop it, it's just going to grow back..."

The two of them looked at each other.

"I guess," said Ken slowly, "that's why the bright woods need us. They need people on our side to keep an eye on things, to make sure that the dark world stays weak."

They sat in silence for some time. Outside the rain could be

151

heard drumming on windows and roof. Slow rumblings from far away informed of the storm coming. Charlotte ate a biscuit, slowly.

How were they going to do it? In her mind, Charlotte counted the cards that were on their side. Herself. Ken. James. The Green King and the Lady. On the other side, one single entity. One single, huge, mind-bogglingly evil thing, lumbering around the caves, and slowly being fed until it got larger and larger.

Glad to get out of their respective houses on such a gloomy day, Charlotte and Ken's mothers were happy to make the trip to the museum. Mrs. Enright declared it a brilliant idea, called Iris Stone and they arranged to go to lunch at in town for hamburgers and ice cream to make an afternoon out of it. Ken's sister Sara was spending the afternoon with friends, and Mrs. Stone decided to take the car so she could pick up her daughter afterwards.

Later, the foursome made their way up the steps to the Museum with bellies full of ice cream, Charlotte leaning on her Mum and still limping a little and wearing one of her Dad's slippers on her still slightly swollen foot. The rain was showing no signs of letting up, and they were all a little damp on their entrance.

Charlotte looked around with interest. She hadn't had much chance to see things on her way out with James the previous morning. Back so soon. She was pleased. In the entranceway to the old manor were the ticket booth, coat check, and a stand selling postcards. To the right was a small tearoom, and to the left the doors that led to the corridor which split and went around in a square, with rooms leading off from one side and a magnificent room in the middle. At one end of the big room were two smaller rooms - more in the way of large closets. Stairs to the cellar had been built from one of these rooms recently, since the house had been turned into a museum. The original entrance to the cellars was from an outside door, now not in use.

All the rooms had been left with their original furnishings. Some pieces were antiques, over four hundred years old, along with paintings, drapes, and carpets. A window into historical England. The family had lived for so long in one house that there was no sense of it belonging to one particular era, although since it had been acquired by the town in the early 1900's it had more of a nineteenth-century feeling to it.

The ballroom in the middle was full of displays of photographs of the town through its history, old birth registers and antiques. At one end was a modern-looking library containing copies of the town's newspapers on microfilm, going back almost two hundred years. The town had always kept copies in the library and most of them had been preserved well enough to be photographed. There was a copy of the birth and death registers, some magazines, written histories, anything anyone could want to know about the town.

This was where Ken had spent a lot of time the previous few summers, and he wanted to drag Charlotte off to look at it. Charlotte was having no part of it.

"Come on, Charlotte," he had said. "You've got to see the old files. Everything about the family is here. They have a whole section devoted to the family, files and files of stuff!"

"Ken, we've got to get to that passageway. This place is so huge we can lose the mums for at least an hour. I've got my watch, let's go!"

"But Charlotte, maybe there's something here. We've got all afternoon, there's no hurry. We can't just disappear right away. Come and see this!"

Just then the mums appeared at the other end of the ballroom and waved. Charlotte and Ken looked at each other. Ken smiled. Charlotte shrugged her shoulders. They waved back, and then wandered over to the library, moving slowly so Charlotte could keep up.

Ken knew where to go right away. The librarian recognised him and came over smiling.

"Looking for anything new about your family, are you?" she smiled.

"Sort of," Ken replied. "Why, is there anything new?"

153

"As a matter of fact, there is. Funny how we found it, too. There's a cat in here to keep the mice down and it went missing yesterday. This morning we went downstairs to look for it and found a stack of old boxes had fallen over in the basement."

Charlotte drew her breath in sharply and looked at Ken. Had the corridor been discovered? The librarian didn't notice the exchanged glances as she was rattling on with her story.

"We lifted the boxes to see if the cat was trapped underneath. It wasn't there but we found an old box that was in the wrong place; probably been there for years." She noticed their faces and assumed they were wondering about the boxes. "We have lots of archive boxes down there; old files, letters, things we don't display. Most of it is rubbish to be honest, reminds us that we need to look through it all one day. Anyway, we found a really old box full of bundles of old letters. They're pretty fragile, some of them are extremely damaged. If you like, I can take you up to the restoring room. We've called in an expert so that we can photograph them – we're very lucky that he was able to come today. He's done a lot for this museum," she rattled on, "he's retired now, I think he was happy to have something to do…"

So they hadn't noticed the entrance to the corridor. The peeling wallpaper must have hidden it – it had only been open a crack, after all.

"Where was the cat?" asked Charlotte casually.

"Oh," said the librarian. "We haven't found her yet. I am a little worried."

It sounded as though the corridor probably hadn't been found. Charlotte was really glad.

Ken was already accepting the offer to see the old letters. Mrs. Stone had bought Mrs. Enright over to the library.

"There's all sorts of things in here," Mrs. Stone was saying. "Ken spent days and days here one summer. You know we're descended from the family don't you?"

"Yes, Charlotte told me. You're very lucky to have your family history all set out for you. I've been wanting to find out more about this town and our families – we're all from around here too you know. This is wonderful." Mrs. Enright looked around happily.

"How's your foot Charlotte?" she asked.

"Not too bad, thanks," answered Charlotte, and it did indeed feel a little better - in fact, the scratches made by the thorns had healed so fast, they would soon be completely gone.

Ken and Charlotte left their mothers going through the old scrapbooks with promises to meet them in the tearoom in another hour.

One hour. Charlotte looked at her watch. It was two-fifteen. So, quarter after three, maybe three-thirty if they pushed it.

The Librarian led them up to the upstairs room where the letters were being examined, and introduced them to Mr. Landers, a tall man with glasses and thinning grey hair. He ushered them inside and warned them not to touch anything. The room smelt clean, and it was cooler than the rest of the house.

"It's air-conditioned in here," said Mr. Landers, noticing Charlotte's involuntary shiver.

"Climate controlled to stop paper from decaying. The town is very fortunate to have such a good museum." She noticed that he was wearing gloves.

The box was sitting on a table. It was open, and Mr. Landers had a letter open in front of him. It had been unfolded and was almost torn along the fold. The paper had yellowed quite a bit but the ink was still clear. It was sitting on a little tray under a special light.

"Can you read it? What does it say?" asked Ken.

"It's rather interesting, actually," said Mr. Landers. "It's from someone in the town to Edward Porter the fifth, talking about some trade they made. Threatening him, actually."

"Who's it from?" asked Ken anxiously. Mr. Landers looked over at him. Ken was bent over as far as he could, trying to see the paper.

"I know you. You're Iris Stone's son, aren't you?"

155

"Yes," replied Ken, puzzled.

"I've known your mother for long, long, while. Is she here?"

"Yes," said Ken.

"Good. Perhaps I'll pop down and talk to her." He smiled at Ken. "So that's why you're so interested. Didn't you do that article on the family we have downstairs? You did, didn't you?" he asked, smiling at Ken's blush. "Quite a well researched piece of work, that. Especially for a lad your age."

"Ken, you didn't tell me you'd written anything!" said Charlotte.

Ken blushed. "It wasn't much. I just wrote down everything I'd read and made sort of a history of the family. I did it for myself. Mum went and showed it to the library and they made a copy of it for the files, sort of a little book," he looked at the floor and then back at Charlotte and Mr. Landers. He smiled. "Well, so who's the letter from, then?"

"Aha. Well, it's from a Mr. Harold Singer. Wonder who that was? Rings a faint bell..."

"I know who that was," said Ken excitedly. "The Singer family built my house. They lived there for ages until the last generation had a fight with Edward Porter about land in the woods. They were some of the people that disappeared while he was alive. It was all very strange. We were just talking about them."

"That's right. Well, I can see your mind is as sharp as ever. You'd make a grand historian, you would."

Ken blushed again.

"Well, we knew this box existed, but we haven't been able to find it. Every time I get called in here for a new find I wonder if it'll be this box. It got lost a few years ago, you see, when we did some renovations."

Charlotte interrupted: "Where does all the new stuff that you get called in for come from?".

"Well, there are lots of old families in this town. Lots of old houses, too. Sometimes when people die, either the family or the people that buy the house will find old

156

newspapers, letters, photographs, things about the town. They get donated to the museum, and inevitably they're falling apart. I get to pick things out, see if they're worth saving, and if they are, I try to save them. Simple."

"Where else do you work?" she asked.

"Oh, I don't any more, not very much. I used to work for the county, actually. Sometimes I still do the odd thing, there's usually enough to keep me busy."

"You must know a lot about the area," Ken remarked.

"Quite a bit. And this is my hometown, so I take a special interest. I've often hoped that some of the last Porter family's secrets are around somewhere. We have boxes of letters to and from the family going back a long time, but this is the most interesting generation, the last one. They were pretty shady characters, the last Porters. Not to cast aspersions on your history, young man," he added to Ken in apology. "No offence meant."

"None taken," said Ken amiably.

They looked at the old letter for a while longer, and the two of them left. Ken was extremely curious as to the contents of the rest of the box. There was almost no correspondence in existence from Edward Porter the fifth, it had all been compiled into the one box prior to cataloguing and then lost. What existed was already quite exciting. There was a letter to a friend that implied that he had done something to the Singers and which referred to another letter that hadn't been found.

Charlotte was anxious to go down to the basement. There were quite a few people in the museum. The first day of the summer holidays and it was raining. Many parents had had the same idea and there were lots of children in the museum. All were younger than Ken and Charlotte, and they didn't see anyone they knew.

They went back downstairs to the ballroom, and skulked around trying to locate their mums. The two women were still in the library, which meant they hadn't even begun to explore the whole house. Charlotte and Ken crept along the corridors to the entrance to the basement.

The door to the stairs was propped open.

"For the cat," guessed Charlotte.

They checked down the corridors. Nobody came around the corners, and they slipped unnoticed into the room and down the stairs.

There was a light on in the basement. The walls were lined with shelves, and there were plenty of piles of boxes; everything looked as it had done on Friday.

Charlotte tried to remember where the door had been. She walked over to a place where the boxes didn't have much dust on them, and sure enough, there was the cracked wallpaper, and just visible the square flap that James had cut over the handle.

"Here it is!" she called in a low voice.

Ken came over.

"Funny. I wonder why the boxes were in a heap. We restacked them, left a little path."

"Are you sure?" asked Ken. "Maybe you were so tired you just thought you stacked them."

"No way. It was painful with my foot. I remember. Uh-oh." Charlotte's face fell. "Maybe someone else found the door." She let out a little squeak. "Maybe that thing found it's way though..."

Ken's heart leapt. But no. "No. If it had come though we'd have known. Even if it looked like a man..." He didn't sound too certain at all. They stopped. "Well, if it came through, then it's gone. We'd feel it if it was here. It'd be long gone..."

Charlotte was not convinced. She held the scarf she had knotted around her neck tightly and felt safer. "We've got to move these boxes again."

They bent down. There weren't that many boxes and they moved them carefully, once again opening up a neat pathway. Charlotte's foot throbbed a bit, but not too much. They finished in a matter of minutes.

Ken reached under the flap and turned the handle. Hearts in mouths, they opened the door and squeezed through.

"Blast!" cried Charlotte.

"No light," agreed Ken.

"Wait. I left my torch here. Somewhere. Just in case." She fumbled around and found it in the corner where she'd left it. The light was strong and they peered down the tunnel. A sudden noise came from beyond the light.

A creak, and a soft padding sound... Something moving towards them. Charlotte let out a squeak and bounded back towards the door, Ken behind her, chuckling.

"Charlotte!" he said, "it's just the cat. The cat, Charlotte." He reached out and grabbed her by the shoulder, shaking her.

She stopped, and turned her light back down the passageway. Right on cue, the cat stepped into the lit circle, stretched, and meowed at them. She sighed in relief.

"Well, that explains that. The cat must have jumped onto the boxes, and the door was open enough for it to get through. The boxes probably fell over onto the door and closed it. Lucky the daft thing wasn't hurt. Good thing we found her, she'd have been stuck down here without us."

The cat purred around their ankles, Charlotte picked her up quickly and gave her a little squeeze, suddenly very glad to have found her. She was rewarded with a little cat-lick on her cheek. With the mystery explained, they turned to the second door that opened into the underground tunnel and they opened it with higher spirits.

Not knowing that a sealed room can gather fumes, the two of them were unprepared for the blast that hit them. They staggered back a little. The air cleared after a moment or two, and they shone the light inside, cautiously.

Inside was what looked like an office. An old desk sat in the middle of a room about fifteen feet square with a wooden chair beside it. There was an antique filing cabinet in place on one wall, and the rest of the walls were covered in shelves, books, and little knick-knacks. They crept around together. Everything was covered in a thick, thick carpet of dust and most things were barely visible.

They looked at each other, both of them hugely excited. Ken pushed some of the dust aside on a shelf. Here was a knife identical to the one that Ken and James owned, along with matching sheath. There was a sword with the same wood embedded in the hilt. Then a statue, lots of statues.

There were piles of clothing on the shelves, each with a label. Charlotte pulled off the dust and examined a label.

"John Dean," it said. The one next to it said "Anna Dean". And the one next to that said "Harold Springer". There were nineteen such shelves. The ones in the back had some rather gruesome artefacts along with the crumbling clothes. The first two had a skull nestled in the centre. Five more after that had small earthenware jars, neatly labelled "Last remayns of" and another name. After that, there were just the clothes. Whoever had made this room had had a fiendish imagination and had kept careful track of what looked like murders. 19 shelves. 7 sets of remains. That left 12 people. Charlotte immediately thought about the things in the woods... Could they once have been human?

At least it seemed as though their suspicions were right: the Porters had gotten rid of their enemies, and it looked as though some of them had been led down the tunnel to the dark woods.

Ken and Charlotte moved closer together, instinctively. Poor people. Led naked down a gloomy corridor into dank caves and... Charlotte started shaking, holding on to her scarf for comfort. Ken reached for her hand and she took it unthinkingly. Unwilling to turn their backs on those shelves, but interested in the rest of the room they walked towards the desk. In the middle of it, under the dust they could see a large but thin book, closed. The cat curled around their ankles still, seemingly un-hungry. Judging by the small tracks and the droppings in the dust of the corridor, the cat had had a happy night's mousing, unaware that it had nearly been walled up.

Ken reached out with his free hand and lifted the cover carefully.

"Diarie of the Hystorie and Spirits of the Thorn Woode" was inscribed on the title page in a flowing hand, hard to read.

"This is amazing!" cried Ken. "Mr. Landers has to see this."

"You can't let him see that!" said Charlotte. "What if he believes it? We don't want people knowing about it... that would be awful. It comes through people's minds, you know. The more people that know about it, even if they think it's made up..."

Ken looked at her, comprehension dawning. "Right," he replied. "I know how badly things I've read have scared me, even though I know they're just stories."

"We should take it, brush the dust on the desk so you can't tell anything was there. Then we should just go," advised Charlotte. She was beginning to be anxious to leave this dank cellar and go back to the warm upstairs, with real lights. She'd even rather go outside into the rain.

"No," said Ken. "We can't tell Mr. Landers about the book, but we have to tell him about the room. We'll tell him we thought we could hear the cat and we went exploring. Let's just walk up and down the corridor a bit, make more footprints, cover your old ones."

"No - the tunnel is really long. We'll just say it was us..."

"Let's just walk a little way, anyway."

So the two of them left the room reluctantly and walked for a few minutes down the corridor and back so it looked like the only footprints were theirs. They took the book, brushed the dust smooth again and gave the desk a critical look. It looked smeared, so Ken sat on it. "We'll just blame me," he said with a grin, his trousers covered in dust. They hid the book under Ken's shirt and went upstairs. He put it unobtrusively behind an exhibit and they went to find their parents. They found Mr. Landers and their mums talking by the tearoom in the front. They burst in.

"Mr. Landers, Mr. Landers!" cried Ken excitedly.

"What is it lad? The whole place is going silly. Miss Peterson was in here just now all excited because the cat came back, covered in muck and dust."

"That's what I wanted to tell you!" puffed Ken.

"Well, I know already," answered Mr. Landers.

"It's not the cat, it's not the cat. We were walking by the door to the basement and we thought we heard it, so we went downstairs to look."

"Oh yes?" asked the older man curiously.

Ken stopped to catch his breath and Charlotte picked up the story.

"Well, we heard it coming from behind a wall, behind some boxes..."

"Probably the ones that fell over before," interrupted Ken.

"Yes" said Charlotte, continuing, "it was behind a wall, and we found a secret door. The cat must have gotten through it somehow and got locked out. There was a handle in the wall, we opened it and there's a tunnel down there. That's where the cat was."

"Goodness!" said Mrs. Stone. "Whatever were you doing snooping downstairs? Don't you know any better? You should have called someone from the museum..."

"No, no," said Mr. Landers. "It's alright. It's Ken's house, after all," and he grinned. "I'm sure the museum doesn't mind. What was down the tunnel?"

"Nothing really," said Ken, "only there's a door to another room, with, well, I think you better see for yourself."

"Well, I'll talk to someone and we'll go down."

The expedition to the basement was quite an occasion. Mr. Landers and the museum's director went down together with Charlotte and Ken, with lots of light. What they found took them by surprise, and delight. Mr. Landers got a gleam in his eye.

"We have to work fast. Now the room has been unsealed things are going to decay fast. I'm going to call my office and see if they can spare anyone. This is the find of the century for this town. And," he continued, talking now to Ken and Charlotte, "we owe a lot to your fine hearing, you two. If either of you are at all interested in what we find here, come and see me and I'll show you around. Not for a couple of days, mind you. Lots of people are going to be interested in this."

They went back to the tearoom. Ken walked to the postcard

booth and bought a colouring book of the museum 'for Sara' he claimed. More importantly, he got a bag large enough to hold the book they had found. He took a stroll and recovered it from its hiding place, then joined the ladies in the tearoom for a sandwich.

On the way home, in low voices in the back seat of the car, Ken and Charlotte agreed to meet later on to look at the book. Ken took it to his house to read by himself. He had lots of hiding places for it, and by rights, he reasoned, it was his book. He was worried that it would start to fall apart, and had picked somewhere dry and dark for it.

That evening the rain stopped the two of them from visiting each other. Charlotte sat in her room, looking out across the fields in front of the house and thought about James. What were they going to do? Her phone had been buzzing for several days and so she settled in on her windowsill to kill time answering text messages; although she really wasn't very enthusiastic about her old life any more.

Clouds covered the sky, thick and low. It was still raining. Although the rain had let up slightly by the time they left the museum, it was only temporary. There were slow rumblings in the hills. The woods looked dark and impenetrable. There was a storm coming.

Charlotte and her Mother loved storms, although her Father hated them. The barns blocked the view from the living room window in one direction, but they could still see across the valley and over the woods on the far side. Charlotte had a good seat from the west window in her bedroom, but they decided to sit in the living room with mugs of cocoa if there was going to be lightning.

After supper, it really began to rain. Charlotte was still sitting upstairs waiting. From her window, she could see the storm climbing across the hills. The first flash had been a long way away, and each succeeding flash was a little brighter. The storm stalked across the countryside on long, spiky legs of lightning. It seemed to be moving parallel to her house, not actually coming much closer, but moving across the horizon. The sky was black.

She went downstairs, and met her mother halfway.

"Just coming to get you," said Mrs. Enright. "It's shifting to the front and it's going to be good. Milk's on the stove right now, your father's watching it for me."

"Goody! Lightning!" laughed Charlotte.

Over in the Starlings' top field, the cows were still lying by the sheds. They'd spent most of the day lying down, chewing their cud in the shelter of the walls. They weren't very happy. Tails twitched. Noses were lifted into the rain and dropped back down. Number 211 shifted uneasily from her seat on the outside of the herd. She watched the woods intently.

In the barns, the Starling men were making certain all the smaller animals were safe inside. They checked everything, until they were sure no storm-panicked animal could break out. Once everything was done, they hurried back inside to a roaring fireplace and a movie on television.

James sat in the warm living room feeling uneasy. He hated storms. He had a feeling about this one. It was going to be bad. Very bad. The weather forecasts backed him up. This storm was unusual. It was centred quite locally, and showed no signs of blowing itself out. It was centred, he noticed on the TV Weather map, right over the town. In fact, the spiral of the clouds was suspiciously circling exactly over the woods.

He hunkered down further into his chair, thinking.

Ken was making great discoveries. As the storm began to grow he was bent over his desk carefully puzzling out letters and words. The book was fragile but not badly so. The pages were dry and yellow but weren't crumbling.

It was not a big book, but the writing was hard to decipher. The story, as Ken unfolded it, was basically as follows.

Ken and Charlotte had been right about the origin of the tunnel. The Porters had found the caves and dug a bolthole for themselves so they could get in and out of their house without anyone knowing. Eventually they had stumbled into the 'Thorny Woods' and discovered the thorns right away, losing a member of the party to the bushes in the process. They didn't quite understand how to get there at first but realised they could get to and from the thorns through the tunnel.

After leaving someone there to explore, they also discovered that the woods changed everyone who stayed there for too long and they devised their plan for ridding themselves of enemies without leaving any traces.

They had also discovered something else. There had been a big tree at the mouth of the caves. This, guessed Ken, was the stump that was there now. It had burned down a very long time ago. Ken realized that Edward Porter (the fifth), who had written the book, was transcribing history. He hadn't found the woods, his ancestors had and they had taken a team of workers in with them, hoping to build a secret house. This is part of what he read, translated into modern English:

"Shortly before they entered the woods a deer appeared. The men rushed at it, being hungry, and chased it. They shot it and rather than leave it behind, carried it through with them. This was in Edward II's time, and his story seems to be beyond human belief, but I will narrate it as he told it on his deathbed. As the dead deer entered the Thorny woods it started to change. Smoke began to rise about it. It assumed the form of a young man, strange to the sight. The men all swore it to be green of skin, but they did only see it a short time. The smoke became fire, and the fire leapt out and consumed the deer-man, then spread into the thicket, rushing out of the cave door and burned the tree. In a very few seconds the tree did fall over the cave mouth. They had to dig their way back into the caves, losing one man to the thorns."

'So,' thought Ken, 'that's what happens when the two worlds meet. Even something dead from the Green woods can't cross over.'

165

He kept reading. These centuries' old explorers had discovered many things about the dark woods. They had discovered what Charlotte had already experienced - namely that if they stayed in the woods for a long enough time their skin would become greyer, start to droop and sag. They had tried to set build their house in the woods but the man they left in charge there went mad.

"The first week they went back to see how work was going. They found Crabshaw in an excited state. His face was by now quite dark, and his features barely recognisable. He had barely touched the food left for him, and seemed to have an unholy fear of water. As if the evil in the woods could not abide the things of natural life - not food, not water, not the body itself. He begged to come home, as he was much frightened. He was left there with more supplies and the following week the men returned. He had done no more work on the building and did not recognise anybody. He did not look human at all, he resembled a demon, with black, ropey skin and long thin limbs. His gums had shrivelled and his teeth were long and sharpened. When water was thrown on him, his skin smoked. It was believed he had joined the devil in his work. He was left there. Curiously enough, among the men who crossed over to the dark woods, there were some who remained unaffected by the place, and it was these men who hunted and slaughtered the deranged Crabshaw."

Water. Ken was excited. This may be of use to them in their battle against their own monster.

Outside, the storm raged. It was late, and pitch dark outside. The lightning had moved, he realized.

Charlotte and her mother had noticed the path of the storm, too. It was circling around, counter-clockwise. Soon it would pass out of sight of the windows and around behind the house.

In the dark woods, the storm was immense, powered from under the ground itself. The dark woods were the centre of the storm. The point of origin. In the caves, unknown to anyone else, the thing was raging, insane and with no sense.

166

It was still a blob, big and clumsy, able to move, able to feel vibrations but nothing else, yet it was absorbing everything.

The monsters in the woods that Ken and Charlotte now knew used to be people had cleared the entrance to the caves, ripping aside the thorns. They made their way to the blob that used to be fog, and one by one were absorbed, taken in. As each one was absorbed, the mass grew a little more coherent. It started taking on form, gaining power.

It sorted through its mind. The memories of the pitiful beings that used to be people were almost gone, but there was one of them which was still a crystal clear ball of hatred. One shining piece of information glittering amongst the chaos in its brain. It knew. It remembered the tree... a book... a deer... The blob's clumsy mind fumbled for clarity but there was none to be found. It had only scraps to go on, but now it knew that there was a way out and, after the last of the blackened and twisted people were absorbed, it began climbing out of the caves.

Chapter 13

Ken, Charlotte and James each went to bed around ten that night. They each slept soundly for seven hours. They each dreamt a similar dream, and they each woke up at five, knowing what they had to do.

Ken had fallen asleep over the book, lying in bed. His mother had looked in on him and merely turned out the lights, not seeing the dusty volume beside him on the sheets.

Ken woke up. Outside his window, a terrible wind was blowing. He sat up sharply and listened. It was cold. He reached out from under his covers and grabbed his shirt from its permanent spot beside the bed. In the stormy light, it was glowing strongly. He yanked it over his head, got up, and padded over to the window clad only in the shirt and his pyjama trousers.

It wasn't raining. Just cold and violently windy. He could still see flashes of lightning and the thunder sounded as if it was right overhead. No rain though. The ground was sodden, the stars were shining through holes in the clouds. Most curious weather, he thought.

He got dressed in his glowing shirt in the dim light and put the old book in his knapsack, wrapped in a plastic bag. He reached under his bed and dragged out an old blanket, and a couple of sandwiches. When the storm had started he'd had a 'feeling', and gotten together some supplies. He had also added a few things from his bedroom cupboard that he had a sneaking suspicion would come in handy. He listened to the house, then lifted his window and dropped quietly to the roof of the shed below. The cold seeped through his jumper and his jacket. A clammy, slimy cold. 'Like bathing in iced jelly,' he mused. He let himself down from the top of the shed and set off across the fields, not noticing his mother looking out her window after him.

Inside the house, Mrs. Stone sighed. She had wanted to talk to her son. Wanted to explain something to him, and now it was too late. Ken's packing hadn't gone unnoticed and she had realized immediately that he was following in his great-grandfather's footsteps. She knew far more about Ken's family than he did himself, and had been waiting for the inevitable ever since the shirt she had made him from the fabric they found in the attic had become virtually attached to his skin. She hoped he'd be alright and, unaware of the dangers her son was approaching, she whispered a silent something to the dark house and tiptoed back into bed beside her sleeping husband.

Charlotte was already dressed when Ken arrived outside her window. She had kept her torch after their trip to the museum, and it was in a bag along with extra clothing - just in case...

Ken saw her at the window before he'd even started searching for a rock to throw. He made shivering motions at her, and when she crept down she was warmly dressed and carrying an extra jumper for Ken. Her scarf glowed brightly around her neck, and Roger padded silently at her heels.

"He's behaving very strangely. He got up as soon as I did and he hasn't made a sound. He even followed me into the bathroom. He's got the strangest look in his eyes...

Roger did indeed have a strange look to him. The dog had a purpose. No gallivanting around, no sniffing of walls. He sat down, mouth shut, looking at them intently, waiting. Charlotte handed Ken the extra jumper.

"Thanks," he acknowledged, "you didn't have to, it's me own fault I didn't wear enough clothes."

"You're going to be lying down on the ground again, aren't you?" Charlotte pointed out.

"Got that right," he agreed, glumly. He'd much rather have been right on the spot, but he knew his job. He'd been preparing for it all his life. "I bought along an extra blanket, too, but the jumper'll come in handy," he said, pulling it on and then putting his anorak back on over the top.

The three of them began descending the field below Charlotte's house. Halfway down, they stopped, aware of something missing.

"Have we forgotten anything?" asked Charlotte. Roger sat down, patiently.

169

"Nnnooo... Not that I can thi... James!" remembered Ken. "I have a feeling we're all in this together."

They set off on a diagonal track down the hill and then back up the other side, towards the Starlings' farm. They had just crossed over the stream at the bottom when two dogs bounded down the hillside, scaring them half to death. Ted Three and Bo, with James doubtlessly close behind them.

"Ho! Charlotte! Ken!" called James. His words were trapped by the air, condensed. His torch was barely visible. The sounds filtered down as if from a great distance. The air was sucking things in - noises, lights. The two at the bottom hailed back. They stood and waited back on their side of the water.

"Check this out!" said Ken to Charlotte suddenly, waving his torch around.

"What?" she asked.

"Your light, the light..."

"Oh. My batteries must be dead. I put new ones in tonight... I must have put the old ones back by mistake..." moaned Charlotte.

"No, look at the bulb, it's fine. Mine's doing the same."

They squinted into the ends of their torches. The bulbs gleamed brilliantly, blinding them for a moment. They played with the beams for a while.

"Look. Look at the beam. As soon as it hits anything it fades..." Charlotte noticed.

"That's not all" interrupted James, climbing the stile and panting. "Listen" and he shouted. "HAH!"

There was no echo. In fact, although he yelled as loud as he could, it carried only as far as Ken and Charlotte before fading out. Charlotte thought back to the day her and her father had yelled across the valley and the echoes had been thunderous. Thunderous...

"Something's eating the sound," said Ken. A look of fear crossed his face. "And the light."

Ted Three and Bo were sniffing at Roger happily. The three dogs looked at the humans playing with the lights, and Roger gave one small 'woof'.

170

"Strangest thing…" said James. "When I got outside, they were waiting for me. Wouldn't leave me be..."

"Me Mum's dogs were at the door too, little fools. I wouldn't let them come though," said Ken. "They're too small."

The three humans looked at each other, and at the three dogs. Something terrible was happening. Fear clasped each heart. Fear mounting, mounting...

"Hey!!" yelled James. "Hey!" and he started dancing around like a fool and laughing. Giggles rose through his throat. "Look at us! Fearless blooming monster hunters!"

Ken looked disgusted, Charlotte puzzled, and then amused. She understood and immediately started leaping around and yelling with James.

"Ken! Ken! No fear Ken! Nothing to be afraid of but fear itself!" she laughed. Laughing was becoming easier. The torches flared up a little, and Ken got the hint. The more frightened they were, the more likely they were to attract whatever it was that was sitting in the dark 'Thorny Woode'. If sitting was what it was doing...

Ken began to chuckle, then to laugh, in earnest. It's hard to be frightened when all your friends are happy and laughing, hard to remain glum. The dogs seemed to catch the feeling, lifted up their tails and started running in circles, letting out small yaps once in a while.

They set off towards the gap in the hedge, half running, half dancing, singing rounds of 'Row Row Row Your Boat' which turned out to be the only song for which all three of knew all the words.

As they approached the gap, they slowed down, and became quiet. Charlotte bent down and rubbed her throbbing foot.

A group of green people met them in deer form. A soft voice sounded in their heads.

"James and Ken, you both are carrying knives. You must give them to us."

James and Ken looked at each other.

"We aren't going to use them on anyone..." began James,

but he was cut off by the voice.

"It isn't your intentions that are in question here. You are going to cross over into our world and the knives will stop your passage. You will get them back once you leave the clearing."

The boys presented their knives, identical except for the carvings on the hilts. They put them at the roots of a tree that was indicated, and the world rippled, changed.

All around the woods was a wall. A very high stone wall. Set into it were the same gates that Charlotte (and indeed, all of them) had seen in dreams. They checked the grass and trees, which were moving with a life of their own. They were in the bright woods.

As they approached the gates, a small group of green people silently encircled them, guiding them inside safely. They walked down the path until they reached the clearing.

Inside the clearing there were so many of the green people, that they filled it to overflowing. The whole place was lit with a beautiful, unearthly glow. The three humans were ushered into the centre, in front of the Green King and the Lady. The dogs wandered over to where a large group of other dogs had gathered.

Ken looked around carefully, knowing that he may never again have the chance to enter this world.

The clearing was full of dogs. Dogs that lived in the bright woods, and other, normal dogs like Roger, Bo and Ted Three who had managed to get outside and make their own way there. They were all standing restlessly and looking intently at the Green King.

There were others in the clearing, people that looked human, with skin that was not green. Amongst these was the old man whom Charlotte finally realized must be Ken's mysterious Great-Grandfather, somehow still alive in the bright woods. Ken had noticed him too, she realized, and was staring outright at the man, who was smiling back.

"We are glad you came," said the Green King, his voice rang loud in the silence. Thunder could be heard in the distance, but there didn't seem to be any rain. "Before

172

tonight begins, there are things that must be said."

James shifted on his feet. This was bringing back uncomfortable memories for him, memories of a time many years ago when he had been in this same clearing.

"The three of you have been chosen to help us in this troubled time. You have all been picked for various reasons, and we have been watching you for years now. We are certain of our choices in this matter, and hope that you will join us."

Charlotte opened her mouth to protest, but a shake of the Green King's head stopped her.

"You, too, Charlotte. It is no coincidence that you moved into your house, or felt drawn towards these trees. Once, years ago, a young girl much like you came to these woods. She loved the woods, and was loved by them. She resolved that when she was older, she was going to live here forever. When she grew up and got married, she had a woman child, and she bought that child to live here, by the woods. That girl was your mother, although she barely remembers anything of this. When we knew of our need, we called her home, and she came. Your Father too. He grew up in this area. Your families have been known to us for centuries. Yours too," he added, looking at both Ken and James.

Charlotte was standing with her mouth wide open. She wasn't the only one. Ken had been eyeing the older man at the edge of the clearing, and bells had been going off in his head. The old man got up and walked towards him after a nod from the Green King.

"You have recognised me, I see," the old man said.

"Um..." stammered Ken, not certain he believed what was going on.

The man laughed. "Well, I am, indeed, your Great Grandfather. My mother was a girl from the woods, my father a man from the town. My skin looked human enough for me to pass as such, provided I got lots of sun..." he chuckled. "Not a pirate, not from far away at all! I was from right here, right in the woods. And I returned here, also, when old age began to take me. Time flows differently on

173

the body here in this world. It doesn't stop, but a man has many many years to live in this leafy shelter. I have kept a close eye on you, my boy."

Ken didn't know whether to laugh or shut-up. Being face to face with a notorious ancestor isn't something that happens often, and he elected to stay quiet and listen. The man continued. "I spent many years in that hut, it had a roof in my time... But in all those years, I was never needed. Now the need is great, but I am old. Your sister feels no yearning towards the trees, but you have spent your whole life in here. I don't doubt you'll elect to stay with us. Not if you are truly my own Great-Grandson."

"No, I mean yes, of course, I mean... I'm staying, here..." Ken trailed off, he had no words for it, but he had made his point. James was looking at both Ken and Charlotte with a little awe, and not a small amount of sadness. The Green King turned to him and spoke.

"Lastly, James. You have been part of the woods for a very long time, James. Neither your mother, nor your father, nor any member of your family was born here, but you were."

James became silent. He knew he had been adopted, although it was something he had not told anyone. His mother had had a terrible time with Ted and couldn't have another baby. The Starlings loved him and he felt closer to them than most sons to their real parents. They were the only people he had ever really cared about and he had never thought at all about his real parents. The Green King's words were only beginning to sink in...

"You were born to humans living with us here in the woods. They are, I am sorry to say, long dead. While we are immortal, humans here are not, but their life spans are lengthened considerably and you would have had to spend years as a small baby. After the accident that killed your parents the decision was made to send you out into your own world. We had no idea what harm would come to the mind of someone trapped as a baby for such a long time, you were only a year old before they died."

Charlotte and Ken stared at James, open-mouthed. A real

174

changeling. Practically, anyway.

"Our influence outside the woods is greater than you might think, and when the Starlings began to think of adopting a child we arranged that you be that child. We may," he added, "have even had an influence on their decision to adopt." He stood back, twinkling slightly.

"But what about that time I went missing for so long? Why can't I remember anything?" James had plenty of questions. This all sounded like something he may have heard before and he had a sneaking suspicion that the Green King's 'influence' may extend to his own memories.

The Green King was chuckling a little. "You always did manage to ask the right questions. Even as a child. Yes, we undertook to educate you at a young age, and you were at that time full of questions about your parents. You demanded to be allowed to live with us and for a short while you did stay – but you belong in the other world. We thought it best that you not remember anything. The only reason I tell you this now is because there must be nothing hidden from you, nothing that may raise questions in your mind during what is ahead. If you are going to take this work upon you, all of you," at this he turned to Charlotte and Ken who were looking at James in total surprise, "then you must know that it is forever, for the rest of your lives, wherever you might go. You must know everything about yourselves, and about us."

James felt a tingling in his head, and there came a flood of memory. He remembered the days spent in the bright woods, remembered how homesick he had been, and remembered the terrible sense of loss he had felt once he was returned to the 'real' world without those memories. For a brief second, other memories came, blurry memories without form or logic, of being hungry, full, tired, awake, but then they sank into his mind and he could only remember the memory of them.

Charlotte and Ken both felt a ripple touch them, although there was nothing hidden from them. The three humans stood for a moment in the clearing, feeling happy, contented, peaceful. They felt a deep sense of kinship with the people of the Green woods, and all three were willing to dedicate their lives in whatever ways they could to help.

The Green King asked, "Are you all willing to take on these jobs?" and one by one they nodded and said, "Yes."

The Lady, who through all this had been standing still and watching, raised her hands above her head, and a white light began radiating from her body. She spread her arms wide, and a beam came from each hand. The beams of light met, swept across the air to the standing children, and enveloped them in brilliant and dancing light. The three of them instantly felt a deeper sense of connection. For that moment, they could feel the thoughts of every person in the clearing, of each other. For an instant they glimpsed the possible futures ahead of them, their lives flew open and then closed, and then the light faded and they were left only with the memory of that moment, and a lasting feeling of well-being and rightness. Charlotte felt a tingling in her foot, and to her surprise realized that she couldn't feel any pain. She jumped up and down cautiously. Her foot was completely healed.

The Lady was smiling at them. "Now," came the voice in their heads, "there is work to be done."

Ken cleared his throat. "Um, I think I may have discovered something."

The Green King and the Lady looked at him curiously. Ken explained about the book he and Charlotte had found, and when he explained the part about water making the things smoke, everyone burst out with questions.

"Right!" said Charlotte. "There's no water at all in the Dark woods."

"Even the river's dry," butted in James.

The Green King raised his eyebrows. "See, I knew you'd come in handy, young Ken," he chuckled. "Now, we just need to arm James with some water..." he stopped and sighed.

"I've got something," said Ken, and out of his knapsack he poured a pile of water pistols, including one that fired several bursts at once. James started laughing. Everyone else

176

joined in.

"Looks like I'm going fully armed!" he chuckled nervously. Ken had filled the pistols from the outside taps on his way to the clearing, and James spent a few minutes making sure they were all full and tucking them into his belt. "If I even need something to make me laugh over there, this should do it!"

Charlotte picked out one for herself just in case, and then the Green King stepped forward, holding something out to James.

"Years ago, James," he started, "you had an interest in the crossbow. Have you done any shooting since?"

"Not much," James admitted. "I haven't touched it in ages and ages."

"Well," said the Green King, "take this," and he held out a beautiful crossbow, and a quiver of straight arrows. "It was carved from wood out of your world, so it will be able to cross over into the dark woods. We don't know anything about this beast, but you may be able to do some damage with this. Try to blind it if you can."

"Thank you," said James, looking admiringly at the weapon. "It's beautiful."

"And accurate. We have blessed this bow so that it will shoot straight even if you don't. Just concentrate on your target. It's your gift."

The Green King looked at Ken and Charlotte. "Charlotte," he said, "you have had the gift of your scarf, however we have something else for you. "

He turned to the Lady, who was still silent. She reached behind her and pulled out a long, thin stick, handing it to Charlotte. It was made of some hard wood, and carved all over with symbols. At one end a crystal was set into the wood so smoothly that Charlotte could barely see the join. The other end was wound tightly with cloth. A wand!

She looked up at the Lady and smiled, and the Lady was smiling back at her. "One day I'll teach you the symbols," she laughed. "For now, it will help you channel the energy that I will be sending you. Later, you will learn how to use it

177

yourself. If you have to go to help James, you must leave it behind with your scarf, otherwise it will stop you crossing into the other world." Charlotte rather hoped she wouldn't have to do that.

"Ken," the Green King continued, "your gift has not been finished. It is something that will see you through your life, and enable you to see into the worlds without having to go to the hut. Tonight, however, you must go there. And, it's time to start, NOW!"

The clearing came alive with urgency. The thing in the dark woods was moving. The storm was raging, and although there was no rain, the lightning was circling around and around the woods, getting closer and closer.

Up in the Starlings' field, Bluebell, cow number 211, had stood up and was watching the woods intently. Slowly other cows stood up, and soon the whole herd was moving slowly down to the gate at the bottom of the field.

Everyone feared that when the storm hit, the monster would gather enough energy from it to cross into the real world. Once it had made the transition, there would be little to stop it. Ken had left for the ruined hut already having had his knife, with its hilt from blackthorn grown in the dark world, returned. Soon he would report back to them all to let them know where the thing was. The Green King had left on some mysterious mission, followed by all the dogs, yapping excitedly. James and Charlotte were staying behind, waiting to find out where exactly the thing was before James crossed over.

James had been worried about his ability to cross over on his own, it was something he wasn't usually very good at doing. He had no reason to worry, however as the crossbow would help him to do it, and now he had taken the job as guardian of the dark woods he would certainly get enough practice. He would however, never again be able to enter the bright woods without the concentrated aid of the Green King or the Lady and he would probably suffer some discomfort even then. He fingered his knife nervously.

Charlotte also found herself able to cross between her

178

world and the bright woods with almost no concentration needed. She would stay in the real world and she was James' only help if he needed it. She was prepared to have to cross into the dark woods, however much that made her shiver with disgust. She looked around the clearing and saw a few familiar faces, Gaua included. The other girl was smiling.

James had the most dangerous job. Since he, of everyone involved, was the only one crossing into the dark woods, he had to lead the thing into the real world where everyone could do battle. Armed with the crossbow and the water pistols he only felt a little better.

Ken's voice sounded suddenly in their heads: "It's already outside the caves! It's having some trouble with the thorns, but it's forming itself into a giant! It's got legs and sort of arms, and it's changing fast. It's sucking energy in from everywhere! James, it's on its way to the other side of the woods, towards the bridge. If you run, you can make it to the junction of the paths and distract it before it gets much further. It's slow right now, you'll make it."

They wanted to get the thing out of the woods and force it into crossing into the human world, where there would be many of them to fight it. James ran until he reached the entrance to the caves, and checked with Ken to find out where the thing was.

"James, it's much closer than we thought! It's about twenty feet in front of you but it's not moving right now, it's doing some more changing. You can probably get its attention easily. Don't get too close!"

James crossed over and was amazed at how easy it suddenly was. He saw the thing immediately, standing with its back to him, making hideous groaning and grunting noises. It was about eleven feet tall, and as James watched it changed shape, squishing down and out for a moment, becoming very short and fat. When it stretched back up, its legs were a little longer and had knees. Its arms undergoing similar changes, twisting and elongating, hands were forming.

James yelled. "Hey!!! Hey fatso!!! You!!! Ho!!" The thing

179

didn't seem to hear him. He wondered if it had ears. When it still didn't move, he walked a little closer to it, his heart pounding madly.

When he got close enough, he crossed into his own world for a moment and picked up a rock. He crossed back, and threw it.

Instantly, the thing turned around.

Its head was lumpy and uneven. It had eyes, eyes the size of footballs, greyish eyes with no pupils, no irises. They worked, though, as the thing fixed its gaze on James. It took a fumbling step towards him.

James, for the first time in his life, felt real fear. All bravado gone, terrified, the boy stood rooted to the spot before a voice in his head broke him out of his stupor.

"James! Run, you dolt!" It was Ken. James heard him, and crossed back to the real world. The memory of that thing lurching in his direction horrified him. He realized that if it had somehow gained the ability to cross over, it would be right on him at any moment. He turned and ran.

"Where is it, Ken? Where is it?" James demanded.

"It's moved towards you, but it's confused. I don't want to go poking around in its head again, but I think you have its attention. If you stop where the paths meet you'll be far enough away."

James ran back to the t-junction, turned and crossed back. The thing was standing still, a few feet closer than it had been. He waved and yelled again. It lifted its head and looked around, blindly. James threw another rock and it walked unsteadily in his direction.

As he watched, its eyes changed, the centres darkened into definite pupils, and it focused on him. It really was changing fast. The surface of its head was bulging in and out madly. Suddenly, a gash under its eyes opened, a great big black hole, filled, James realized, with rudimentary teeth. Teeth the size of shovel heads, pointed and getting sharper all the time.

It lurched forward another step, and then another, and another, and just as James was about to cross back, the thing

180

fell on its face, upset by its own weight.

'Some monster!' thought James. 'More like battling a toddler.' He picked a water pistol out of his belt, and cautiously walked to where the thing was flailing around like a turtle turned upside down, trying to stand up. He levelled his pistol at its head and shot a perfect squirt of water.

What happened surprised him. Where the water touched its skin, the thing burst into smoke. It roared, and flattened right out into a puddle of black ooze. Almost instantly, it gathered itself back into the shape it had before, but this time, standing up, reaching out for James. A small hole under its left arm smoked for a second and closed.

James crossed back, horrified. The thing wasn't solid yet. Until it was, it would just keep changing shape. If you lopped off its head, it would just grow another. Who knows where its brain really was? Certainly, every time the thing changed, it was able to move faster, see better... James started running.

"Ken!" he yelled in his head. "Gotcha, mate," called back Ken, "start running for the edge of the woods. Charlotte's going to be waiting for you. I think the Green King's got something up his sleeve, too."

James hit out for the edge of the woods.

Back in the clearing, Charlotte was talking to the Lady.

"You are my link to your world. You must wait for James by the edge of the trees. Go, with my blessing and be ready for anything!" The Green Lady's voice was soft, like water in her head. Charlotte felt again the wash of well-being run through her, and she started to leave the clearing. A hand tapped her on the shoulder. Gaua.

"I'm coming with you," said the girl. The two of them crossed over to the human world, and they ran down the path to the gates of the woods, Gaua in her girl form, leading the way.

On the way, they met James, panting for breath. He'd raced for quite a ways before stopping, realizing he was going to have to cross back so the thing could see him. He waved them on.

"Give me another five minutes, I'm on the way. It still can't cross over," he puffed. They waved and left him there.

In his hut, Ken was keeping a careful eye on the monster. It still hadn't quite finished its transformation, but it had changed quite a bit in the fifteen minutes since James first saw it. It now had fully developed arms and legs, hands and feet, fingers and toes, with claws still growing and sharpening. Its head was firm, and it had two rows of sharp teeth, each one a foot long and growing. Its eyes were huge, and its vision was extremely accurate. Huge ears had sprouted from the sides of its head.

It was lumbering forward again, not quite certain what to do. Ken called James and James crossed back to the Dark Woods about ten feet away, waved, and then to the thing's eyes, he disappeared as he crossed back yet again into the real world. It ran towards him, and he reappeared another fifteen feet away.

"Hey!!" yelled James. The thing started running, James crossed back, and ran towards the edge of the woods. It was easy. He hailed the girls: "I'm coming!! Tell everyone to get out of the way!!"

The group of deer by the gates scattered to a safe distance. Charlotte and Gaua moved off the path, and waited with stopped hearts, holding hands for comfort.

James appeared in the dark woods one more time, this time right at the end of the path, where it exited into the field. Ken warned him that the thing was moving fast, but it didn't prepare him for the reality. He thought he had gotten far enough ahead, but the thing was almost on him. He shot it with blasts of water from two pistols. He got it right in the eyes, and it lurched to a stop. Ken, in his hut, sensed the monster's confusion. Over the woods, the lightning had become more intense. It shot bolts across the hills, lighting up the interior of his hut. It started coming thicker and faster.

Still there was no rain.

In the field, the flashes of lightning illuminated the people, casting short shadows. The clouds began to whirl into a knot, gathering together.

The cows, led by number 211, were pushing their bodies slowly against the wooden fence posts at the bottom of the field.

James ran out into the field below Charlotte's house, swung the crossbow around from his shoulder and loaded a bolt while the thing was still howling. Its face was smoking, but it was healing over fast. It stood still for a moment, long enough for James to fire the bow. He concentrated, and the bolt hit it square in the centre of the forehead, but it didn't even seem to notice. It started towards him. Suddenly the clouds let forth a huge bolt of lightning. Ken sensed a change in the thing as it sucked the full force of the lightning bolt into its body.

In the real world, the bolt of lightning disappeared instantly - it didn't hit the ground, just passed right into the dark world. James ran towards the edge of the woods and nearly hit the wall of thorns. He crossed into the real world, came barrelling out of the gap in the hedge and once safely through, crossed back.

It launched itself right through the thorns surrounding the woods and towards him. He emptied both water pistols through the thorns, and reached for the last one in his belt. Where the water had hit it, its skin dissolved a little, but it was obvious that the water pistol was not enough.

Charlotte and Gaua were poised and ready. Charlotte had her water pistol ready, and Gaua and the rest of the Green people were waiting in their own world, each one with a loaded crossbow.

As they waited, they saw James appear, running. Ken's voice came screaming in their head telling them that the water pistols weren't enough, and then there was a blast of foul smelling air, and the thing appeared in front of them, howling and running for James.

With the energy it had gained from the lightning, the thing

183

had crossed over by itself. As soon as it crossed over, another bolt of lightning crashed out of the clouds and hit it. It grew. It grew and then threw itself at James, who was careening down the hill towards the stream. How had it known to cross over??

What happened next happened almost too fast for Charlotte to comprehend. First, the monster reached James, grabbed onto him and James started screaming. It had him by the leg, and his leg was smoking and cracking. He screamed in agony, and then blacked out into unconsciousness.

Next, a volley of arrows hit the thing. Green people were darting in and out of the human world in their green forms, careless of who may be watching, and firing arrows of wood from their trees at the thing. Where every arrow made from wood grown in the bright woods hit it, it burst into flames. More lightning struck it. It began to grow and grow, like a balloon blowing up. Soon it was so big that it overshadowed the field. It became as big as a house, then as big as a skyscraper, then it was bigger than the field...

Everyone except Charlotte and James went running for cover.

In his hut, Ken was watching everything. He could sense some strange things from the Green King, but they weren't as important as what was happening in the field. He saw the monster grow. Although it was still only fog-like, whatever it touched began to burst into flames. Soon, the ground was on fire, and the flames were creeping towards the woods. There was nothing for him to do, he thought, but to enter into its mind. The last time he had done so he had almost lost himself. This time the monster was older, more developed. Less chaotic. Was it safer? Or more dangerous?

There was no time for him to decide, and without further thought he leapt into its head. Blackness. Chaos. Fear, hatred, everything was still there, but now there were new things. Fragments. Memories that it didn't even know that it had. Men, women, buried deep in its mind. Trapped in there, a part of it. Memories of so long ago... no TV's no radios, no jet planes, no computers... firesides, a woman's hands in front of her, washing a floor... a man walking through a workhouse where many people worked over looms... another man, milking a cow... a child playing in a house... old memories... whose?

Ken sifted through the wealth of buried information, looking for one thing. He had to find it quickly. No time to dwell on the other minds he found in the thing's head. He delved deeper and deeper into the dark whirlpool. He felt himself again being dragged inside. His presence in the thing's mind had stopped it as before, and now the thing had stopped howling and was teetering like a giant balloon over the field, not moving. He felt it searching through its mind for him.

Ken stayed always one step ahead of the thing's questing thoughts until he found... himself... himself... Himself clear as a crystal. Himself as an old, twisted, dying man. An old man full of envy and hate. An old man crouched over a desk in a candle-lit room... wait a minute... he had it.

Edward Porter the fifth. Edward Porter, his Great-Great-Grandfather... Edward Porter who had written the history of the woods. Edward Porter who had not died after all, but who had walked into the woods looking for eternal life.

The whole story was there. He had been poisoning himself for years with minute amounts of the poison from the thorns and had thought that it would make him immortal. He had built a house in the middle of the clearing, provisioned it and planned to use it as a base from which he could cross over and rob nearby villages for years until he had been forgotten, when he would come back immortal, and still with enormous wealth. He and his wife had faked his death and used the ashes of one of his victims in his place, paying off the undertaker. His wife, glad to be rid of him, had lived the rest of her days with the secret, not knowing where he was or what he had done, just that he had gone. Edward Porter the fifth had been one of the leathery half-humans in the woods.

Perhaps Edward Porter hadn't realized the price he would

185

pay for his eternal life – madness and disfigurement, trapped in the woods by the poison in his veins. He had roamed the paths in the 'Thorny Woods' searching for the way out for the last hundred years, trying and trying, needing something stronger to return him to his world.

Who knows whether or not he caused the fog to gather itself together? One thing is for certain however and that is that Edward Porter the Fifth's twisted hopes were driving the monster back into his own world.

Ken pulled out of the thing's mind. As he did so, he felt it grab at him, start to pull him in. He felt the old man, waken and croak. Ken began to choke and flail around on the floor of the hut... the link between he and his ancient relative was too strong... he couldn't get free... he was trapped... fading... fading... The thing began to move. Ken had stopped it for long enough that it was on fire all from the arrows, but it was now melting back into its giant form, sealing over each arrow hole as it came.

With the time Ken had purchased, Charlotte had gotten ready for her turn, grasping her wand in her hand and felt a ball of heat gathering in her stomach, which spread all through her body. As it spread, all her hairs stood straight on end. It spread through her lungs, through her mind, through her toes, her legs, her heart, her shoulders... She felt her arms lifting without her willing them to do so. She was standing in the same position as the Lady had been in the clearing earlier, arms spread up and wide, head thrown back.

As the monster was re-forming, a beam of white light poured from the end of the wand. Charlotte felt like a riverbed, or an electrical cord, the vessel for movement and power. Light flowed out of her in great waves. The beam became brighter and brighter, then soared up and hit the sky.

The clouds were now full of rain, rain just waiting to fall, rain being held back by the thing in the field below. The Lady's energy came through Charlotte, hit the clouds, charging the rain with light. Glowing white drops fell from the sky, and wherever they hit the ground, flowers began to grow, plants writhed out of the soil, beauty grew in

186

abundance everywhere. The fires on the ground sizzled, smoked, and went out. Wherever the drops hit the monster, steam rose. Flames began to pour from its body. Another bolt coursed through Charlotte, and this time it hit the thing, right in the middle of its belly.

The giant monstrosity burst. It burst into little pieces that ran howling into the dawn, pieces that once had been people; innocent, everyday people. People who wanted nothing more from life than to live it happily and peacefully, and who had been condemned to an eternity of witless horror in the dark woods. People who had been used, but not yet completely destroyed. Most of them fell, then got up and tried to run away. Some of them slowed down, began to sit down in the flowers now blooming in the field. Some of them just howled and howled. Some of them, with no trace of humanity in them leapt on the onlookers, trying to tear them into shreds.

Just then, a horn sounded. A horn that blew a long, clear tone, a note that rang inside Charlotte's head and not in her ears. Out of the wood rode a tall figure with horns, riding on a horse, or was it a half-horse half-deer? Or half-man half-deer? It was surrounded an enormous pack of excited, howling dogs. They ran after every leathery human and rounded them up like sheep. At the bottom of the field, the cows broke through the fence and started up the hill, climbing up to the top gates.

The Green King and his pack rode down all the people. He tore them off their victims, blowing his horn and setting them free. He walked to the ones sitting in the flowers and touched them gently. Puffs of smoke rose from each one as he set them loose from their bodies. Grey, leathery things dissolved, became light and disappeared. As each one rose from the remains of their bodies, laughter and singing could be heard over the valley.

All except one. One of them had fallen to the ground and not moved until this moment. When the horn began to sound, this one had crept quietly away, and was now running, running.

Edward Porter was finally free, and he knew who and what he was. And he was not alone. With him he carried the mind of his Great-grandson. And he was heading for the ruins.

"Come with me, we can be the masters of everybody!!" the old man was saying to Ken. "With your body, my mind, my immortality, we... I mean you... can have anything I... we... you want..."

The old man's greed was horrible. Ken tried and tried to get free, but he was trapped. The old man had spent years and years in the dark woods with only his madness to keep him company, and Ken had only just found his own strengths.

Behind the old man, a horn was sounding. Before he could reach the ruined house, a dog nipped at his left foot. He kicked, but another dog grabbed his other leg, then another grabbed his thigh, another grabbed his right arm, and then his left... He struggled but the tide of dogs was too great. Soon he was buried in a mountain of growling dogs. Small dogs, big dogs, hunting dogs, pet dogs.

Inside Edward Porter's mind, Ken struggled to free himself. The old man was so distracted by the attack that he relaxed his hold on the boy for a moment. Ken felt his own body for a second, grabbed onto it and yanked himself out.

The dogs surrounded the withered thing, growling through their teeth. Around them was a bigger circle made up of large, soft bodies, the cows, snorting and stamping but otherwise calm. The Green King rode into the middle of the circle as Charlotte and the Green People watched. It was hard to look at him. His antlers gleamed faintly in the dark, like Charlotte's scarf and Ken's shirt. When he reached the monster that used to be Edward Porter the fifth, he gestured with his left hand and the dogs moved away, out of the circle of cows. Porter lay on the ground, his evil old mind confused and dim.

"Edward Porter," intoned the Green King, "you have been an evil man." Porter made a choked sound in the back of his throat, the sound of someone who hadn't used their voice for hundreds of years. He wasn't prepared for this. He didn't know who it was talking to him, but he knew he was afraid.

What the Green King said to Edward Porter in his head and what Porter replied was not known to the others, but after a long time Porter bowed his head and for a moment looked less like a monster and more like an old man. The cows had moved forward and stood almost touching their noses to the two figures, shielding them from watching eyes.

A ball of light formed around the group. It got brighter and brighter, blinding the watchers. Then, just as Charlotte had to look away from it, it shrank back smaller and smaller, until it was inside the circle of animals, sending long cow shadows across the field.

Finally, the Green King rode out on his own, a small ball of light in his hand. The cows moved back and started wandering across the field, touching their noses to the injured. Behind them on the grass was a slowly dissolving grey husk. The dogs raced in to sniff it over, but there was nothing left for them to do, as it disappeared. Charlotte watched as the Green King released the ball into the sky, where it rose, and slowly faded out.

Ken lay for a while, dizzy and confused, but elated. They had won. The monster had been destroyed.

He hunted through the worlds for his friends. James lay unconscious on the field, his leg mangled. Charlotte was walking towards him, and while Ken watched, the Lady washed light over the fallen boy, and his leg became whole again. James stood up, dazed and confused but whole. Light washed over everyone in the field, dogs with broken teeth, Green People with burns, everyone was healed. Even Ken felt a touch of healing energy, and his strength returned.

Ken stood up, and left the house, running for the open field, where, if anyone had been watching, the strangest sight was in progress.

Vines were growing everywhere, flowers and fruit sprouted where there had only been grass before. Green people were dancing, laughing, eating. Two, and now three young humans were yelling and screaming joyfully while packs and packs of dogs chased each other in circles, and a man with a deer head galloped on horseback across the woods to his Lady waiting inside – or was it a large grey stag?

The cows filed patiently back through the fence and up the hill to wait by their barn. It was nearly milking time, after all.

Chapter 14

Everyone met in the clearing. Ken and James were helped across into the bright woods for the second time that night, and they found a celebration in progress.

Makeshift tables had been set up, laden with fruit and drink for the battle-weary, and every one of the green people were there. Ken's Great-Grandfather was there too, and when Ken entered the clearing, he greeted him warmly.

"Well my boy, welcome home! I suppose you've had quite enough of grandfathers for tonight..." he said, raising his eyebrows. He and Ken laughed together a moment. Gaua and another girl came around with goblets of wine and juices, and Ken and his ancestor each took one.

"Here's to you, Ken," said the old man.

"And..." said Ken raising his juice, "to you too!" and they laughed again.

"Well," said Ken's Great-grandfather, "you have done the job for which I am now too old to have managed, and you have done well. I hope your services aren't ever required again, but the state of your world is unfortunately going to affect both our world and the other, and I fear we may need you again sooner than later. For now, however, it is time to celebrate! And, we have something for you, nearly finished now."

He led Ken over to one of the trees in the clearing. Hanging from one of the lower branches was a beautiful coat, just waiting for large buttons to be sewn on. The buttons were hanging on the same tree in Ken's own world, unable to cross over. The Green King took Ken into his own world for a moment to look at them. They were carved out of wood from the thorns in the dark world, and each one had a little scene on it. One had the ruined house, one had the clearing carved on it complete with deer, one had a map of the woods, each intricately done. They crossed back. The coat was made out of more of the green fabric, but in a thicker weave. The pockets were deep, the collar high, and it was lined with a light but thick material that kept in the heat.

It was absolutely beautiful.

"This will act in place of the hut. Wear it wherever you go, and you will be able to see in and out of all the worlds – although not get through. Anybody who wears this will be safe from the dark world."

Ken was virtually speechless. "Thanks, thanks a lot," was all he could say.

The Green King walked over to them, and asked them to sit down and listen for a while. They each grabbed a handful of fruit and picked a comfortable root to sit on - Charlotte grabbing her old favourite.

"You have done us a great service. Without your help we may have been in great trouble. Certainly your world would have been thrown into terrible times. If more people had gone missing the woods would certainly have been levelled."

James, Ken and Charlotte all looked puzzled. They didn't know about the town's plans for the woods. "Well, we generally know what goes on in your world quite accurately. This we found out by reading a newspaper, I'm afraid. Nothing exciting."

The thought of the Green King sitting down with the local paper made Charlotte smile. "So," she asked cheekily, "do you get the paper delivered?!"

Everyone laughed at that, but the Green King just smiled and shook his head. "Nice idea, though," he answered.

"Actually," piped up Ken's Great-Grandfather, "I take a walk into town once in a while."

The Green King continued, "but I have things to say to you before tonight is over."

The night was over, actually. The sun was over the horizon, and a pleasant breeze was wafting through the trees. Overhead, the branches rustled gently and incessantly, sending messages across the expanse of green. The clearing smelt sweet and mysterious, and looked astonishing, with throngs of Green people meandering in and out, children out of bed and running around, catching the excitement. Some of the dogs were still in the woods, letting out the occasional bark and chasing each other in the bracken before returning

192

to their homes.

The Green King cleared his throat and raised his glass. "First, a toast to you. Thank you again."

They drank, and he set his goblet on the grass beside him. "You have all taken on very serious tasks in agreeing to help us. We, as I think I mentioned before, are not the only wood like this in the world. If you leave this wood, outside you will find the countryside to be very similar, except that most of the hills are bare."

"In places you will find one tree, perhaps a clump, but most of the trees from our world are now dead, or dying. The trees that remain are all places of power, places where all three worlds meet, and as such they can be dangerous. Energy from your world leaks through, energy from ours leaks out, and energy from the shadow world also."

"These trees have often been places of worship over the centuries, certain groves were held in awe by people who sensed a greater energy, an even more ancient energy than in this world or the other. These groves later became points where the division of the worlds began into the three that we know, and some of the places still exist."

"Across the globe of the Earth are many, many different points. Some are whole woods such as this, others are smaller areas. There are a few that have no trees at all. You will all be able to sense these places, and enter any of them at will. With practice, you will also be able to use them to travel anywhere."

"Anywhere?" interrupted Charlotte. "That would save money on plane tickets!" her voice startled her a moment, she'd forgotten about speaking mind to mind, besides, she didn't even know if the others would understand her, anyway.

"Yes, it would," answered the Green King, "but you must be careful not to use this method of travel lightly. Do you remember, Charlotte, when you found yourself passing out whenever you crossed over to our world? Do you remember that the Dark world would reach out for you and I told you about the area between the worlds?"

193

"Yes," said Charlotte in a small voice.

"Well, this area is the space you must use for transport. Because it leaves you open to influence from all three worlds, you will find that you lose a lot of energy travelling like that. If you do it too often, or for too long, you will eventually find that you cannot do it at all, anymore, and even that your ability to cross between the worlds will be weakened. You will eventually get sucked into the dark land as that one tends to suck in weak things. And in other parts of the world, other monsters like the one we just saw could be growing – although we have not sensed anything as yet. The worse thing that could happen is that you might find yourself travelling and be unable to leave the space between the worlds. You would become a ghost, not existing in any world at all, condemned to travel for eternity."

Charlotte shivered until James piped up with a chuckle: "And then I'll have to go looking for you... again."

"Don't be so cocky, James," said Ken. "Could be you he's talking about, couldn't it?"

"Or you!" threw back James. "Least I'd know my way around..." They quieted down a bit at the thought of being lost between the worlds.

"You wouldn't be much good at finding your way around dead, now, would you young James?" asked Ken's Great-Grandfather, who'd been sitting with them and listening in. "By the time you fell into that dark land, you might have been lost between the worlds for a few hundred years..."

The Green King nodded silently in assent. The three young humans looked suitably impressed by this. None of them wanted any part of the travel now.

"Still," advised the Green King, "if you use it cautiously, you will have no trouble. And you will be using it."

The three looked questioningly at him.

"The three of you, in dedicating your lives to this wood, have dedicated yourselves to the whole world. There are few others like you. This is one of the strongest places, and most of the others have very few people in them. You must all learn as much as you can about your land, about this planet.

You will travel if you like, you will study what you want, go about your lives as you would normally, just remembering always your duty to watch for signs of the dark land gaining power. When you are needed, you will go there. All of you."

"Well," said James, "I was going to stay right here..."

"Wonderful," said the Green King. "But take a lot of holidays!" and he laughed.

The meeting was over. The sun was high, the storm was over, and it was time for them to leave.

They crossed back into their own world, and around them everybody except the Green King and Ken's Great-Grandfather disappeared.

"Will you please give my regards to your Mother?" asked the old man.

"My Mother?" asked Ken. "Why? I mean..."

"Your Mother knows a little more than she's let one to you, son. I'm sort of the family secret, as it were. I've found over the years that there have been occasions where I've had to visit the town, and occasions where I've had to visit the house - sometimes just to rummage through that old trunk, sometimes to put something in it, as I did in the case of that material you're wearing."

"You mean," asked Ken, "that Mum weren't just going through that trunk for no reason... you mean you had put stuff in it for me... recently?"

"That's exactly it. I made you that knife, made James' too. Getting the wood from the dark world was some trouble, too, believe me!"

"I believe you," said Ken, fingering the knife that had just been returned to him.

"You made this?" asked James of his own knife.

"I did. I made it for you when you were with us for that short time..."

"Um... thanks," said the boy.

"My pleasure," the old man replied.

They said their goodbyes, but Charlotte had one thing to ask the Green King.

"What happened to Edward Porter?" she asked.

"Same thing that happened to the others. I released him into death. He was stronger than the others, less willing to go, but in the end even he had to agree with me. He was tired, and without his impossible dream of eternal life he was almost glad to go."

They paused for a minute in contemplation. Just as they were leaving, Gaua appeared running out of the clearing, and gave Charlotte a hug.

"Promise you'll visit?" she asked.

"Try and stop me!" Charlotte replied.

The field outside the woods was still covered with the wild growth that the storm had raised. Vines clambered up the hill, strange and wonderful flowers were open everywhere the rain had touched. The singed parts of the grass were overgrown with new blades, greener and thicker than before. Where the giant thing had finally fallen to pieces there was a large, brown circle, where nothing grew.

"Well," said James, "this is going to have people wondering..."

"Hmm," agreed Charlotte. "Wonder what they'll make of it, anyway?"

They needn't have worried. The strange storm had gathered much attention in the town. As the sun got higher in the sky, the plants went to seed, withered and died, before anyone else saw them. The burnt circle in the field was explained away as a freak bolt of lightning, and the storm as just another strange bit of summer weather.

Old Ted was at a loss as to what had come over the cows, and why they had trampled the fence. "Strangest thing I ever saw," he said.

The first thing Ken did when he had time was go for a visit to the library. Mr. Landers had a couple of assistants helping him unravel the mystery of the secret room.

"It's quite terrible, actually," he told Ken. "There seem to be the remains of several people that were killed, and on the shelf we found a diary of exactly who they were, why and how they were killed, and when. There are also descriptions of people that he sent... Well, that's not entirely clear. They were taken down the passageway and into the caves... Oh!" he clapped his hands, "did I tell you about the caves?"

Ken's heart leapt a little. If the caves were explored by many people, was there a chance they'd accidentally cross over into the dark woods? No, he decided. Evil people had found those woods, evil people had dragged terrified people there. James had crossed over because he had been meant to do so. With the fog gone, interested explorers would only find caves. "No," he finally said.

"Well, there's quite an elaborate cave system at the end of the corridor. It's made the town council hopping mad. They wanted to clear the woods, but they can't dig into the ground very far because of the caves. It wouldn't be safe to build on them. It's good for us though," he continued, "they seem to stretch forever. We've already found a couple of skeletons, perhaps the remains of some of the victims, although one looks like a child. On a brighter note, there's some rather lovely rock formations in this huge cavern down there, also – and some bats. Got some interested geologists spending an afternoon in there right now."

Ken had only ever 'looked' into the caves through James and Charlotte, in the Dark world. He hadn't seen them in his own eyes, and he got the urge to explore them one day.

"Anything else interesting?" asked Ken.

"Not really. Some old account books, the urns... One of those urns is actually empty. Maybe that person got away or something, or it was spilled at some point. There's a few interesting books, some old coins, some lovely statuettes from the period, ought to be worth a little now. It's not that old a room. Still, it is an interesting find. Solves a few old mysteries anyway!"

Now that things had quieted down, the three of them settled into the holidays. James spent quite a bit of time with a girl he had met at school, but mostly he spent time with his friends Tony and Simon.

Ken and his mother sat down and talked about the woods for the first time, mother and son finally being able to talk freely about things close to their heart.

Charlotte spent much time with Rosemary and the girls from her school, swimming and going on trips to the nearby seaside. She got used to feeding the chickens and would walk across the fields with Roger on a regular basis to sit with her favourite cow in the sun. She also spent a lot of time with Ken, who took her on long walks. They explored the countryside for miles around the town.

Once in a while, the three of them would meet in the woods, and meander around happily, sometimes joined by Gaua and some of the other Green People.

The days lengthened and lengthened until the summer solstice arrived. There was a big gathering in the woods, for which James and Ken were crossed once again into the bright woods ("And I thought we weren't supposed to ever come here again!" laughed James to Ken). They danced and ate until late at night, crawled home wearily to their beds and woke the next morning to puzzled family members trying to move them out of their stupors. After this the days once again began to get shorter, and the nights longer. Fruit began to ripen on the apple trees behind Charlotte's house, berries turned red and black through the hedges and were picked for pies.

And so the summer drew to a close.

Lightning Source UK Ltd.
Milton Keynes UK
UKOW051027180213

206437UK00001B/22/P